Pean

with
all my love,

Paul.
Becker.

FALSE TESTIMONY

LENZ
books

CONTENTS

False Testimony   1

The P.A.   21

The White Island   35

The Miracles   117

First published in Great Britain in 2010 by Lenz Books
Text copyright © 2010 by Paul Becker
Cover image ©2010 Jesse Leroy Smith/Paul Becker
Paul Becker is hereby identified as the author of this work in
accordance with Section 77 of the Copyright, Designs and Patents
Act 1988. All rights reserved. No reproduction, copy or transmission
of this publication may be made without written permission.
No paragraph of this publication may be reproduced, copied or
transmitted save with written permission or in accordance with the
provisions of the Copyright Act 1956 (as amended). Any person who
commits any unauthorised act in relation to this publication may be
liable to criminal prosecution and civil claims for damages.
All characters in this book are fictional. Any resemblance to any
person living or dead is purely coincidental.

ISBN 978-0-9564760-3-6

Printed in the UK by: MPG Biddles Ltd.
24 Rollesby Road
Hardwick Industrial Estate.
King's Lynn. Norfolk.

Dedicated to:
AK Richardson
RA Becker
& NJ Hebson

FALSE TESTIMONY

LEPERDIUS' FINAL ATTESTATION TO THE SENATE OF ROME. 239 AD.

Romans. I make my attestation on this the first feast day of Jupiter so that at the same time as all the usual sacrifices are made upon Jupiter's altar, my final sacrifice will be witnessed by all the gods & after my death, my thoroughfare into the next life will be freed from any evil portend, sorcery or ill omens that might otherwise hamper my journey to the Fields of Elysium. I offer up my life to Rome safe in the knowledge that the step I am taking is the best one for the future surety & welfare of her citizens. The internecine struggles for power that would take place were I to live would most surely end in the ruination, the utter destruction of this great city I hold so dear and this I will not allow.

I must, before taking my leave, take upon myself the sins of those others I am leaving behind, those I know to be guilty in certain black matters to have come before this Senate in the last few months. Like the scapegoat sent out into the wilderness, I bear most willingly this necessary mantle of guilt and, by making sworn testimony as to my own liability before those good citizens of Rome here foregathered; will thereby free Rome from some of the terrible sins against her sacred name that are leading to her certain ruination. As this testimony is offered freely upon my honour as a member of the Senate & a true son of Rome I hereby employ this ancient right to bear unto myself the guilt of others. Henceforward all judicial inquiry, implication & suspicion that points towards any persons connected in any way with the crimes I will outline below, shall forthwith be ceased.

That I love Rome few can doubt who know me. I shall therefore, depart this life with a heart free from care, certain in the knowledge that this great city wherein I have spent all my days shall be maintained to the end of time, basking in the everlasting glory of her eternal name....

THE LONG HATCH WITCH TRIAL

This is the Testimony & Sworn Confession of Annabel, alias Annie Brewer as taken by Patrick John Barry, clerk to the court of this parish.

The examinate made strict testimony that around six months to this day within the span of Michaelmas while shee was about gathering sticks on or nearabout the Fairway with her two friends: Mary Elisabeth Clay & Annie Holt (here foresworn) did tell these her friends that shee could at any time, verily summon & conjure forth a familiar or devil which would appear unto her in the form of a browne baby pigge. This sayd familiar whom shee named as My Lord Thumm shee did brazenly attest would be able to empower her of anything shee would desire. Indeed, not longer than two days hence, the examinate professed to meeting with this devil & another familiar who shee named as Methanuel by the inn stable at Cheapside where shee was persuaded to offer up her breasts for them to there suckle upon and this they did, one at each teat & besides took further liberties. It was here saith the examinate that shee was made to kiss the arse of this black devil shee named Methanuel. In return for these her favours & the promise of her Soule to be given over to them at a later time, they did promise unto her all the power shee would have. Shee did also attest that this Methanuel aforementioned was none other than Lucifer himself & upon her agreeing to these terms hee did baptize her with his waters & did place his mark upon her brow, which shee affirmed could still be seen thereon. The examinate also attested that on or around a fortnight from this time shee did meet upon the turnpike by The Great Oak out at Linley one Peggy Robotham daughter of one Henry Peter Robotham, a grower of hops & resident of this parish; returning from Havershall Fayre. The examinate did ask this sayd Mistress Robotham for the tasting of some spiced ale shee had about her person & being refused did offer up a curse on the head of Mistress Robotham, who indeed about ten days hence did fall ill of a most grievous ague & lay abed for many weeks in fear for her mortal soule. The examinate admitted to the making of a picture of clay of Mistress Robotham & burning it upon her settle on or about this time. The examinate did then submit that shee was empowered by her own aforementioned devils or familiars in this matter & sundry other matters of witchcraft, sorcery & general mischief. That one or both of these sayd devils did appear whensoever they were by her summoned to her bed & there did make most wonton sport of her & that shee did then freely copulate therewith. Shee did also affirm most solemnly that shee did make regular nocturnal journeys about the Parish being born aloft by these familiars & that they did oftentimes frequent the graveyard of St. Cuthbert's Church wherein they did meet other imps & devils as well as sundry other witches both male & female & thereafter frolic most wantonly, making water & turdes upon & around the stones & blaspheme against the name of our Lord. The examinate also gave certain testimony that upon one Sabbath in this same graveyard of St. Cuthbert's shee & these other so-called witches did conduct the Black Mass & other blasphemous, ungodly rites that did culminate in the conjuring forth of Satan himself in the form of a Great Black Goat. The examinate did swear most fervently upon the Holy Book to the truth in every part of her statement made above and was publicly burned as a witch the following day it being the March Assizes of Long Hatch.

THE SAN LORENZO *AUTO DA FE*.

Being the Confession of Monsignor Hector-Luis Rodriguez before The Holy Tribune of The Inquisition for the Mortal Sin of Heresy on this day, February the 2nd 1625.

Rodriguez: I do confess here before God Almighty, Christ the Redeemer, Mary Mother of God and all the Holy Saints whose forgiveness I do most humbly crave that I, Hector-Luis Rodriguez, Monsignor of the Parish of San Lorenzo am guilty of the most wicked & heinous sin of heresy. I offer up this evidence of my sin most freely, having not been put to the question & withal being under no duress or pains of torture & do most humbly plead for no mercy whatsoever. Indeed I do believe only the cleansing qualities of the fire will enable my mortal soul to pass up unto my Lord Jesus Christ untainted by this most dreadful sin. That the court should hear my evidence & comprehend my guilt, this I do most humbly beseech.

The Reverend Lord Cardinal of St. Pedro, Bishop of San Lorenzo: Monsignor, I must ask if you are able to offer this Holy Tribunal any direct evidence of your sin? In other words, are you willing to specify in what form your heresy manifested itself?

Rodriguez: Yes your worshipfulness. I am willing and able to prove my absolute guilt in this matter. However, I petition this Tribunal to act most righteously in this affair & to help me in the name of the Lord Jesus Christ to rid myself of this most ungodly taint of heresy. This I also most humbly beseech.

The Rev. Lord Cardinal: Continue.

Rodriguez: Thank you your worshipfulness. My heresy is on four counts. In the first count I did openly question the veracity of certain passages within the Holy Scripture & many of the sacred texts, notably in regard to the Resurrection & the Day of Judgement. In the second count that I did consort with other heretics, Cathars, Lollards & Protestants & did give countenance to these most heretical & liberal arguments against the true Catholic faith: free love outside the sacred bonds of matrimony, the right of priests to marry, the freeing of Catamites from persecution & the introduction of liberalising reforms to the most holy & sanctified tenets of Catholic teaching. In the third count I did call into question the existence of Hell, blatantly arguing for the existence of only an Earthly Paradise. Fourthly that I did question the purposefulness of The Church itself...

The Rev. Lord Cardinal: How so Monsignor? the purposefulness?

Rodriguez: Yes your grace, most especially in the many contradictions embodied in the apparent opposition of the words & teachings of our Lord Jesus Christ to more recent developments; most specifically in the right of The Court of Inquisition itself to anticipate God's judgement on this earth...

The Rev. Lord Cardinal: Monsignor Rodriguez, It is indeed most fortunate that you accept the premise of your guilt in this matter. These are without question the most unholy, most shocking counts of heretical thought & false doctrines I have ever been unfortunate enough to witness. That you are a brother of the cloth makes your crimes even more pernicious & indeed unforgivable. You offer us your evidence as a Christian & yet you delineate the sins of the foulest, most desperate & degenerate heretic. We have no recourse but to apply wholeheartedly the punishment handed down to us by God alone, through the same powers you evidently find so questionable! In consigning your body to flames I pray for your unworthy soul to find peace in the forgiving arms of Almighty God. We shall adjourn to consult & to pray. We shall thereafter pass our condemnation & solemn judgement upon you. Thanks be to God.

Rodriguez: May God's will be done.

CITIZENS OF THE REPUBLIC
VS
THE CITIZEN DUPRÉ

" I, François Jean-Baptiste Dupré do hereby submit to this Tribunal that I have been guilty of many heinous crimes against liberty & against the people of the Citizen's Republic of France in word and in deed. These I here outline:

Firstly, that I did meet with numbers of Royalist spies & émigrés in the employ of Foreign Powers and that I did so with the sole purpose of abetting the escape from the people's custody of other sworn enemies of the Republic.

Secondly, I freely confess that I did plot the overthrow of the Republic with these same divers spies & émigrés aforementioned, that I received various monies thereof & distributed these same monies in several parts to a network of spies & counter revolutionaries throughout France; whereby I did control & direct these said spies & plotters as traitors, assassins and hired-men against the Citizens Republic of France.

Thirdly, I admit that I did travel abroad to London, Brussels &Vienna on several occasions, there to meet with government spies, traitors and other sworn enemies of France to arrange for the furtherance of my personal campaign for the reformation of the Aristocracy & of the Monarchy, and towards the ultimate destruction of the Republic by any means at my disposal.

My crimes are, as outlined above, of the most despicable nature & I defy this court to produce any witness to prove otherwise or to gainsay this testimony. I ask not for any show of mercy or leniency on the part of those here assembled standing in judgement upon me. I place myself into the people's custody of my own free will & I must expect my judgement & thereafter my sentence, to be swift, severe & inflexible."

François Jean-Baptiste Dupré 7 Thermidor. Year II

THE BLAISE AFFAIR

TIMES EDITORIAL.

English Justice being one of the foundations on which the greater glory of Britannia's Rule is founded, we cannot but marvel at its awesome steadfastness & indeed its most inexorable resolve in bringing the wrong-doer in all his manifestations, to task. Let there be no flinching, for no matter how terrible, how disagreeable the crime; it always shall, in the end, be found out, faced down & summarily penalised! In this instance the shameful crime under its judgement is of the utmost scarlet in hue. The crime of sodomy is one of the most dreadful, the most terrible to contemplate & though we must act with true Christian spirit in this matter to try to find in our hearts some semblance of pity for the perpetrators; it flies in the face of all we hold good, decent & clean to let it go unpunished. We hereby print unexpurgated an exact transcript of certain exchanges between Blaise, the Prosecuting Attorney Sir Sidney Boxhampstead & the Judge presiding, Lord Eversham:

Boxhampstead: Mister Blaise. You attest that on the 28th of May 1888, you took up lodgings at Number 17, The Beeches, The High Street, Broadstairs with Lord Wendlesham & Mister O'Shaugnessey? Is that correct?

Blaise: We lived together for a time as friends, in fact for much of that summer...

Lord Eversham: Answer yes or no to the questions if you please Mister Blaise.

Blaise: Just so my Lord. Yes.

Boxhampstead: You say as 'friends' Mister Blaise? Can I ask you to elucidate? Friends in what capacity? May I remind you that you testified earlier to having known Mister

O'Shaugnessey less than a week at that time & moreover that you also testified as to Lord Wendlesham being, in your own words *"a consummate degenerate"*

Blaise: A degenerate, perhaps but also an absolute paragon of charm.

(LAUGHTER)

Lord Eversham: Silence in court. Any more interruptions & I will have the court cleared! The Prosecution may continue.

Boxhampstead: Thank you my Lord. I will at this time present to the Court an engraving made by Mister Blaise during his residency at Broadstairs. Its title, the jury will oblige me by noticing is *"Wendlesham as Lucretia"* & in it the young Lord Wendlesham is for all intents & purposes entirely in a state of undress. Mister Blaise, I put it to you that this is hardly a fit subject for a work of art? A young man who you know to be of dubious moral tone, in the role of a beautiful young woman about to succumb to molestation?

Blaise: I found it amusing at the time. Wendlesham was & indeed still is, a most engaging & for the purposes of art, a most beautiful young man. I believe I was interested in conveying the more feminine aspects of his appearance. Perhaps the engraving is wanting in taste but I believe it is well executed. And very like.

Boxhampstead: My Lord, may I also present to the court Mr. Blaise's diary entries for this period, May to July 1878 in which Mr. Blaise is much more straightforward about his relations with Lord Wendlesham & Mr. O' Shaugnessey. My Lord, if I might be permitted to read a brief extract?

Lord Eversham: Proceed.

Boxhampstead: My Lord, this is an entry from the 4th of June: "*Spent the whole morning in his room with Wendlesham. Quite ravishing. How delightful he can be when he allows himself & really quite well versed in all the arts for one so young*"
Mr. Blaise, surely you will allow that spending the whole morning in the room of a young gentleman who you describe here as "*ravishing*" is slightly untoward to say the least?

Blaise: One must breakfast somewhere Sir Sidney.

(LAUGHTER)

Lord Eversham: Mister Blaise, may I take this opportunity to remind you that this is a court of law & not a comedic Revue at the Drury Lane Theatre. The allegations made against you by these witnesses are of the utmost seriousness in nature & I am forced to repeat that I will not have my Court turned into a makeshift stage for your continual display of witticisms & facetiousness.

Blaise: My Lord, it appears I must apologise unreservedly.

Lord Evesham: The Prosecution may continue its examination.

*THE TRIAL CONTINUED
UNTIL THE FOLLOWING TUESDAY.
THE JURY WAS UNANIMOUS IN FINDING THE DEFENDANT
GUILTY ON ALL COUNTS
(SODOMY, PROCUREMENT
& THE CORRUPTION OF MINORS)*

THE SENTENCE PASSED BY LORD EVERSHAM:
22ND *JUNE 1890*

"Mister Blaise you have been found guilty of one of the most hideous offences to fall within the bounds of Criminal Justice.

In all my long years at the bar I have witnessed all manner of crimes. That one in your position with all the concomitant advantages wrought not only by high renown but also by Birth, Education & a sound Christian upbringing, should drag your family name through the very mire almost beggars belief. You have encircled yourself with a group of acolytes steeped in all the most wretched forms of corruption & allowed this corruption to freely infect the lives of the young & the innocent alike.

The witnesses for the prosecution have proved all this unequivocally but I must tell you now that the most valuable witness for the Prosecution has been yourself. Not only was your testimony utterly half-hearted & riddled with contradictions but on many occasions actually self-condemning.

That you published your guilt for all the world to see not only in your so-called works of art but most flagrantly in the form of a diary and it must be said, the language used therein plumbs new depths of bestiality, depravity & inhuman shamelessness. I repeat, in all my long years spent exercising the law, I have witnessed every manner of crime. Rarely have I been more deeply satisfied by the pronouncement of the Foreman of the Jury.

Mr. Blaise you are hereby sentenced to a minimum of three years Hard Labour at Wandsworth Prison, which is the maximum term allowable in this case. Had there been more years at my disposal you may rest assured, sir, that your sentence would have been stretched to the very limit."

REGIMENTAL COURT MARTIAL FOR COWARDICE OF LANCE CORPORAL NEVILLE COLDWOOD

(Field report: 22nd August 1916. Major Duncan Tanfield McLeish, Kings Own Company 2nd Battalion, The Royal Scots: Officer Commanding Legériere Forward Station).

"The prisoner presented himself into custody at the clearing station outside Legériere very late on the evening of the 20th of August following the advance on the woods on the Poizières-Bapaume Road earlier in the day throughout which the Regiment had played such an active part. The prisoner seemed steady & calm when he was brought before me, though I was forced to have him wait three quarters of an hour while I finished some business with my Quartermaster; Staff Sergeant William McFadden. Upon the completion of my affairs for the day, the prisoner was called into my tent where I was attended by my batman, Private John 'Jock' Harris. The prisoner then reported to me in very straightforward terms the occurrences of the day. That he had fled the advance in no uncertain terms he made clear immediately. I asked him if he realised the consequences of his actions & he quite calmly assented & replied that he fully comprehended the position he was in. I must say that throughout, the prisoner behaved in an exemplary manner & not at all like the usual type of deserter. At this point I had the prisoner dictate & sign a statement to confirm what he had just reported to me. Upon the departure of the prisoner under light guard to the stockade Private Harris immediately informed me that he knew the prisoner, that he had in fact served with him the previous year, before the injury to his throat that had taken him (Harris) out of active service. According to Harris, the prisoner had been mentioned in dispatches following an audacious attack on a fortified machine-gun post during the second day of the Battle of Ypres and was quite astonished by the behaviour of what he described as a good man and an absolutely first rate soldier".

Maj. D. T. McLeish. O/C Kings Own Company
2nd Bn. The Royal Scots. 22nd August 1916

HOLLYWOOD ACTOR
REUBEN "SCOTTIE" MCLOUD APPEARS BEFORE THE HOUSE COMMITTEE ON UN-AMERICAN ACTIVITIES.

Senator: Mr. McLoud are you or have you ever been a member of the Communist Party of America?

McLoud: In answer to that question I would have to say yes, Senator, I have been a member of the Communist Party. I was first approached to join about three years ago while under contact to Fontana Pictures. Since then I have become fundamentally disillusioned with International Communism in all its forms. Indeed I believe it to be the solemn duty of every good American to stop the spread of this contagion at the root-source. That is what brings me before this hearing and before you today.

Senator: Those are indeed sterling words Mr. McLoud but are you able to provide this court with any form of verifiable evidence to bear out what you are saying? As you know we are only able to deal in plain facts and what you are presenting us with here; highly commendable though it may be, is simply not admissible. Do you understand that?

McLoud: Senator, I understand the question. I no longer possess a party card but I am under oath and I hope shortly to present the court with some significant evidence to support what I have been saying in this instance.

Senator: Mr. McLoud, lets not beat about the bush here, are you or are you not prepared to *outline* some details of the activities you were involved in as an active member? To be specific, would you be able to he help this Committee with some facts & figures, dates, places and most importantly, names of other party members known to you? I am thinking in the last case of people involved in the movie industry; ex-colleagues you know to have been associated in any way with the Communist Party? party members known to you? I am thinking in the last case of people involved in the movie industry; ex-colleagues you know to have been associated in any way with the Communist Party?

McLoud: Yes, I could.

Senator: Could you repeat that please Mr. McLoud?

McLoud: I said yes, I believe I could help you Senator, and the Committee, with many examples of fellow professionals, colleagues and friends as well as journalists, policemen, members of the armed forces and politicians who have some connection to the Party, whether in a greater or lesser sense. In fact Senator, before these hearings began, I took the precaution of preparing a list. My duty as a citizen of the United States comes before any personal considerations in this matter. As you will see the list is remarkable in its detail. May I take the liberty of offering it as evidence to the Committee?

Senator: Bursar, could you please pass that along?

McLoud: You will notice Senator that it includes a substantial outline of events, meetings and activities I was involved in; or knew the corresponding parties named within to be involved in, in some capacity.

Federal Defence Attorney Westerhouse: Senator, Mr. McLoud is well aware that much of the evidence enclosed in this document is self-incriminating in that many of the activities outlined therein were attended by him in person. Mr. McLoud waives his rights in this matter, as he believes it to be for the greater good and beneficial to these hearings. An action I trust the court will carefully consider.

Senator: Thank you Mr. Westerhouse. We will certainly make a note of that. The Court will go into recess while we study this document but before doing so; Mr. McLoud, I believe I can speak for the entire Committee in commending your unfailing sense of patriotism.

McLoud: Thank you Senator.

Senator: Thank *you* Mr. McLoud! The court will take a recess and reconvene after lunch.

THE P.A.

The establishment of Frau M. is what one might call strictly informal. She is by no means a stickler for rules of cleanliness or order but things should always be put in their rightful home and at no time should the place be unpresentably dirty. Not at all! Once a week either Vilma or I will run a vacuum cleaner into every corner and pass a cloth over all the surfaces. Glass to be kept free from smudge and dirt, floors spotless. Nothing too severe. This level of informality is a common feature of life on the Z...Strasse and adds to a general feeling of contentment, rocked only by Frau M's very occasional, sometimes dramatic, though usually fully justified, changes of mood.

The house itself consists of cellar, ground floor, first, second and third floors. There is also a small garden at the back, unusual for Berlin. The ground floor serves for the every day functions of the house. There is a dining room where Frau M. breakfasts, a front room for entertaining guests, rather a long hall which leads, via several steps down, to the generous kitchen. The first floor is the beginning of Frau M's private domain (and she is a very private person). Directly at the top of the first flight is a study that, naturally, includes an extensive library. Here Frau M. does most of her research. Next to that is a small day room with a *chaise longue* for relaxation. Then, continuing on to the front of the house is the large studio. This room is kept locked most of the time. Frau M. takes her luncheon in the day room and there is a bell there to call the kitchen when she requires her luncheon to be served. The second floor holds Frau M's living quarters, which are what I would describe as decidedly 'Spartan'. There is a generous bathroom however and a separate dressing room. The third floor is for the servants, including myself, Magda the cook, Vilma, the domestic and

Old Maximillian who has been employed as butler for the M. family for many, many years and who is now something of a jack-of-all-trades.

The structure of my week is simple but the work is constant. I cannot answer for the others, though they all of them seem to be just as exhausted as I am by the weekend! As it is, my *taglich* routine varies little, if at all. I have to meet Frau M. in the morning after she has breakfasted, always modestly, modestly: a hot roll, an egg, soft boiled (for no longer than three minutes), coffee and perhaps a little fruit in summer? I soon got into the habit of copying this routine as I have many other aspects of her life. My mother had always insisted we take a heavy breakfast, arguing for its being beneficial to the constitution. I for one was glad to abandon this practice; it had never agreed with me. I felt that it placed an unnecessary drag on my whole metabolism.

After breakfast then, I will please bring my diary and meet Frau M. in her day room, where she will begin to go over the planned events of the day. *Natürlich*, I will take extensive notes and make suggestions if so required. If we have meetings to go to together then I will call for a cab. Most often Frau M. would have work to do in her studio or some research to complete in the study. If this is the case, I might easily find myself running an errand on her behalf, always depending on what exactly was going forward with her affairs. I might easily be called to a meeting as her representative if she was too busy to attend on her own account, so I have to be always ready with an up-to-the-minute comprehension of every aspect of her diary, her practice and her plans.

I might just as easily have to take a trip to the grocers to settle a bill or to collect some laundry and, in this work, which is as vital as any other, one has to be continually adaptable.

Up until quite recently, at some point towards mid morning, just after her second breakfast at eleven, I would be summoned in to the day room to be beaten, This would (usually) be undertaken with a regular gentleman's walking stick and would not take longer than five or, at the most, ten minutes. In fact, though I say ten, to be completely precise the longest I ever counted was exactly nine minutes and twenty five seconds but that was really something of an aberration as I know for a fact that on that day Frau M. had found me particularly disagreeable.

At fist, I much preferred the routine of these beatings to the more irregular humiliations, certainly in the early days of our working relationship when I did not really understand Frau M. or see things entirely from her perspective, as I do now. With more experience I find I have come around to the opposite view entirely and anyway, Frau M's initial enthusiasm regarding the application of the walking stick soon began to fade. Why it lost it's novelty one can only speculate (I would never attempt to anticipate Frau M's motivations!) but I might hazard the guess that there is only so much one can do with a simple beating, only so far one can go. It must be that one never really gets under the hide of the one being beaten, never truly penetrates to the bone. No matter how hard one goes at it!

The humiliations, however, offer a much more diverse and tangential method of levelling a bothersome underling. The circumstances, if it is well and thoughtfully done, are never the same way twice. One can really get to the meat of an issue and this Frau M. was quick to do. Indeed, this process was very quickly to become what she would now refer to as her *métier* and as one humiliation followed swiftly on the heels of another, I have come to realise that although I rarely have time to conceive of the new set of circumstances that have to be in place to allow one degradation to ramify into the next, miraculously, Frau M. always manages to pick up the thread somewhere. Like a trained surgeon (she never seems to tire), how adept she is at metaphorically revealing one layer of 'smarting skin' after another!

Frau M. is an artist of great genius and significant social standing. She numbers among her set of acquaintance not only prominent film makers, theatre producers and musicians but also financiers, politicians and even the Mayor of Berlin, who is a great supporter of her work. I am proud indeed to be of any service to her. I never thought I was giving satisfaction at first, especially during my early days at Z... Strasse. I knew that there was a particular something about me that irked her and I tried hard to fashion myself into the person I thought she would prefer me to be. However I felt I failed in this endeavour constantly, consistently. Her beatings would see me crying like the merest child, running into corners, hiding under the *chaise longue*, all the while trying to put some distance between my person and the blows Frau M. rained down on me. I was sure that my infantile reactions were infuriating her all the more and I tried hard to summon up the necessary resolve to simply stand there and take my medicine. It is true that I have always had a terrible dread of being beaten. I began to think that I was constitutionally unsuitable and that I had been brought up a coward. Luckily though, when I plucked up what courage I had and voiced these fears to Frau M. she told me that on the contrary, she enjoyed my reactions immensely (this was before she became rather tired of the simple act of physical castigation) and hated to think of my just lying down and letting myself be kicked about like a dog. The whole thing would lack the requisite amount of relish, she said, like shooting fish in the proverbial barrel.

The humiliations had started not three months into my employment. They begin quite spontaneously and were almost jovial at first, involving as they did, then, a random audience of gallery staff, curators, ogling technicians etc.

Dressing-downs, tellings-off for my real, imagined or even invented failings or slights became a regular feature of the job and pretty soon had blossomed out into a regular event at any parties, private views or film premieres attended by Frau M. and myself. I was frankly amazed at Frau M's level of gravitas, her ability to control, to command the attention of her audience, as well as the fecundity of her imagination in always contriving to produce 'the goods' on me. As with the beatings, Frau M. it seems, enjoyed my part in the proceedings. My tears, my wretched pleas to be spared the lashings of her tongue. It all added to the sense of occasion and, as time went on and the events came to be hotly anticipated by an audience appearing in ever greater numbers to witness what would unfold, Frau M. came to believe that she and I had the psychic understanding of trained acrobats.

It is interesting to note that the attitude of the crowd has gradually evolved over time, from polite disgust to, in the end, a gleeful feeling of collaboration, as though just the bare fact of their presence has added a necessary fillip, a spark to the creative flames. As for me, the process became increasingly cathartic. Back when the humiliations had started I was already racked by a feeling of low self-esteem; in a sense, I arrived there with nothing, so the fact that Frau M. made sure that I had even that taken away from me, could easily have destroyed me. But somehow, by peeling away the dead skin and exposing the new, an equilibrium began to be established. I came to feel as though I was undergoing a very public form of psychoanalysis and in many ways I suppose I was. My wounds felt as though they were being painfully cauterized. Painful but increasingly, necessary for my survival.

We have never spoken about the humiliations afterwards. After about a year of it I found I was beginning to wonder, to worry about how much further we could go. How much of me was there left? Frau M. in her approach to each performance (which is what they had now, by logical extension, become) was so expert at never travelling down the same road too often, always keeping me surprised and on the back foot. And yet I felt that once she had pulled down whatever lay at the centre of who I was, whether you call it a soul or not, I don't know. But once that had been shaken into ruins, what then would remain? And what, knowing the rigour and integrity of Frau M's practice, what would be the point of continuation?

The whole ritual had, by this time become an integral part of Frau M's work, to go without it could have the direst consequences. Though, as I said, we never ever talked about it (and though it was not my place to concern myself with such business), I could not help but secretly wonder just how she intended to move the whole thing along, so that it wasn't simply about the dynamic of our 'relationship'. The solution seemed to present itself with the amount of happenstance and intuition that (I am reliably informed) pervades all the very best and most cutting edge performative art. It so happened that we were attending the preview of a large exhibition, at a famous museum in New York; an exhibition that Frau M. was a major part of. Frau M. had begun attacking me in front of a large group of art industry professionals and artists invited for the opening. She was just about past the beginning of her summing-up when, through my tears, I noticed something swirl through the air towards me. I had no time to duck and the half empty can of soda struck me hard against my right temple, drenching my hair in sugary liquid. There was a significant moment of pause as the audience seemed to recognise the significance of what had just occurred. Then, almost as one, the entire audience began to join in the harangue. More missiles were thrown, the guards tried to pick out those who had thrown them as they were concerned about the art works that surrounded the event. For the first time I found myself under a massed physical attack and I have to own, I was absolutely terrified. Punches were thrown and I was spat upon, shaken, slapped down and kicked. Just as the terrible onslaught seemed to reach its height, I began to hear a strange, jubilant laughter circulating among the room. This quickly spread to what felt like the whole audience; sporadic clapping broke out and then built up into a huge spontaneous wave of applause. The whole place erupted. I was able to make my way over to Frau M. who was receiving the applause in great good humour.

Frau M. was very well pleased with her performance and even with my small part in it. She had me sent to a private hospital to recuperate for a few days at her own expense. Apart from cuts and scratches to my face, I had received a broken wrist, lost a tooth and suffered severe bruising around my ribs. By the time I got out and we were ready to fly home, Frau M. had decided to dedicate the entire thrust of her practice towards more humiliations. This was indeed a momentous development and as far as my role was concerned, it began to dawn on me that I had become a much more important figure in Frau M's life. She even came to pick me up in a taxicab from the hospital to tell me of all this exciting news. She also promised to increase my wages by fifty per cent, which I wouldn't hear of but Frau M. had insisted upon. On the flight home, she talked breathlessly about her plans for future performances: the proper settings, scenarios etc. Apparently a well-known American filmmaker had expressed serious interest in capturing one of the humiliations on camera.

I have been truly honoured by her new attentions to me. She has even begun to talk about me in the role of partner, or co-collaborator in the humiliations. For my part I reply that I will always be ready to do her bidding and to help in any way I can. I do have to voice some concerns though, particularly about the violence. I wonder how long my body will be able to sustain physical abuse on this level without compromising my work as her assistant. The hospital treatment could also present new financial issues if she insists on exclusively private healthcare. Frau M. says she has already given the whole matter a great deal of consideration and has finally resolved to hire another assistant to take up my position. I felt shocked to the core and protested most vehemently about this decision. I did not believe, I said, that anyone could know her business as completely as myself. It would take months to establish even a fundamental understanding of her entire operation, her profile and her list of connections.

Predictably, Frau M. soon argued me around, saying that she hoped I would be available (on her new very generous terms!) to aid the newcomer; to help them find their feet and to hit the ground running, as it were. She said that with my expert assistance she believed anyone with some experience in this type of work would be able to establish a handhold and would soon be able to get an overview of all her affairs. I was flattered to hear her opinion of my abilities, especially when she commented that she would never expect anyone to achieve my high level of thoroughness and attention to detail. However, she continued, if I were to agree to act as mentor she believed nothing could be more beneficial to the newcomer than to learn from my experience. She even asked me to help her look through the résumés, to select the best five or six applicants for interview. I was to be present throughout to offer my expert opinion and to help her ask all the right questions.

Of course I agreed to help but had to admit I was laid pretty low by what had been proposed. The emotions flooded over me throughout the next few days. I was truly thunderstruck by the news that I would no longer be Frau M's assistant, that I would no longer be able to help her so directly as I had up until then. While I understood that this whole change was necessary and indeed, constituted an obvious promotion and a substantial increase in my salary, I could not prevent the feeling that a major part of my world, the lodestone, had disappeared forever.

I have tried to concentrate on my part of the work in hand. Frau M. advertised my position immediately and a host of applications began to flood in. As I had promised Frau M. I looked them over, every one. Frau M. had baldly stated that she would only accept the applicant whose résumé and work experience most signally resembled my own. We eventually settled on five applicants for interview including my personal favourite: a slightly more mature woman with a wealth of experience of working at the most demanding levels, including, most recently for the CEO of a major investment bank in Cologne.

However, in the end, Frau M. chose an English girl of twenty-four who, yes, interviewed very well and though admittedly has been working in PR, in the fashion industry for the last year, has little experience as a purpose built PA. Nor did she match any of the criteria I had laid down as a required outline for the applicants. I think Frau M. liked the idea of Gemima's fresh, youthful outlook and could relate to her very much on that level.

So it was Gemima that I would be mentoring over the next few months, bringing her up to speed on Frau M's business affairs. As it turned out though I barely had time to show her more than the rough basics of the operation before Frau M. announced that she, *we*, would be making a unique performance in two weeks time as part of a special Artist's Preview of the Frieze Art Fair, in London. Gemima has really been thrown in at the deep end, in immediately having to arrange publicity for the whole event off the bat. Luckily, I have been on hand to offer practical advice on many matters and the people at Frieze have been very generous with their time and with their help. Notwithstanding that, as the day comes round, poor Gemima is quite burned out and has realised, I think, the full extent of the workload she will be expected to carry from now on. She does seem to get on very well with Frau M. however. Frau M. has never been exasperated with her as she is with me and, to the best of my knowledge; there has never been even the hint of a beating. Even though I had tried to subtly prepare her for that aspect of the job, it seems to have never become an issue.

What with having to help Gemima as much as possible, I had not had a chance to look at a paper all week and was therefore wholly unable to realise the full level of publicity that the Frieze event has successfully generated. Now, as I sit down the evening before the opening, I realise with some horror, that my name and photograph had at least equal footing with Frau M's. To be quite candid, I am deeply ashamed. I am never anything more than a helpful bystander and I cannot see any justification for my inclusion in Frau M's limelight; Frau M is the artist, not me. All the articles under the headlines and photos are highly enthusiastic however and I am glad of *that*, if only for Frau M's sake. I am sure she will turn the evening into a huge sensation. She has already spoken about the event in several interviews as the crowning moment; the very apogee of her career and that is enough to make me greatly proud of even the humblest involvement.

We get to Frieze early in the evening and as we head in, the crowds, already gathered for the event, give Frau M. a hearty cheer! The excitement is palpable. The air is quite thick with it! When we get inside I find myself very confused by the amount of people who want to meet me, to shake me by the hand. I don't want to steal any of Frau M's thunder. I have never been one for blowing my own trumpet, being far more familiar, via the dictates of my job, with the blowing of other people's. I find I am quite overawed by the attention and all the unnecessary silliness.

Frau M. has told me nothing of her plans for the evening of course; she always likes to have as much freedom as possible regarding her 'lines of attack' and I am sure her only wish is that everyone around her feels as relaxed as she does. We have been here ninety minutes and she has only just begun her first onslaught. It comes from nowhere and takes almost everyone, including, me by surprise. I notice the audience are stopped dead in their tracks. She has pitched the volume at exactly the right level. As ever, I am immediately terrified. I have become progressively nervous throughout the whole day, perhaps in preparation and yet nothing could have prepared me for the ferocity of this assault. She is 'on a roll'. I can already tell that Frau M. has spent a lot of time thinking about her approach, preparing the way, mentally ploughing the road. She is proceeding to take me apart piece by tiny piece. She begins to lay the foundation with a truly withering assault on my trite, mediocre and nauseatingly insignificant family, in particular the ineffectiveness, the impotence of my father and the 'bigoted, petty bourgeois small-mindedness of my fuck witch mother'. My whole life history seems to unfold before me as she lays out one senseless act of non-entity after another. Eventually she begins to bring her diatribe into the present, laying open my lack of ability in the work she has paid me so well to do. Thank God, she has finally hired someone to do the job with a spark of vitality whose imagination can meet Frau M's on some sort of fundamental level, not some half-dead, withered up old broiler hen. It goes on from that point, following a much more personal line of abuse.

As she nears the end I find I can hardly hear what she is saying anymore. Not only because I feel so deeply upset but also because many of the audience members have began to join in, quite spontaneously. Huge whoops of approval are echoing around the building, interspersed with bursts of applause and more screams of vitriol. Even I, under attack from all sides as I am, can begin to discern a new feeling of elation emanating from the crowd. Some kind of mass release, a catharsis just like mine.

The first blow comes from a woman I recognise as a minor sixties Pop Art painter. She describes a wide arc with her white handbag that ends with a vicious crack at the back of my neck. There it is again, I feel it even through the shock and pain, that same a moment of quiet when the audience sees and recognises what is happening, that somehow a line has just been crossed. Now a young gentleman in black trilby and moustache punches me in the mouth and several others who can reach me begin to follow suit. Slaps and punches are coming now, thick and fast as well as spittle and wine in my face. There are so many people around me, wanting to get at me that many of them are kept at bay by the tightly packed crowd. Those closest start to bite and to butt at me, being unable to free their arms. My clothes are being torn to pieces. The blood is pouring down my face along with the tears as I scream, like an idiot, for them to stop but more and more people are trying to get at me, to strike at my face. I try to shield myself for a moment of respite but my arms are soon pinioned to my side. Looking up for a second, the mob seems to part and I catch sight of the figure of Frau M. She is quite relaxed, talking to a well-known curator and drinking a glass of what looks like her favourite: Prosecco. As far as I can tell her part in the performance is at an end. Now the crowd closes up again and I sense a new resolve pass among my attackers. Punches fall on me from all sides.

I have begun to lose consciousness and feel myself falling to the floor; hundreds of pairs of feet begin to stamp on me as hard as they can.

THE WHITE ISLAND

A turd! Black as molasses, smooth and perfectly formed and yet there, at its head, a half circle of bean seems to stare up at me like a rudimentary eye. The eye of an accuser, a home-made spy! Inside my head, in every different compartment: treason. My brain is like the state of Russia and a traitor lies in every cell. I have to try and gain control of myself. This is important. Last night they came for the Bulgarian on the floor above - its my bad luck to be located just across from the stairs. *Imbeciles!* said their leader, *this is the 9th floor! I told you the Bulgarian was on 10!*

The lift is erratic. I haven't the nerve to leave the flat. I don't want to miss them when they come and (of course) I don't want to answer either. What would happen were I not to be present, not there at that moment? Would the whole machine break down? I mean the system, the paperwork. I don't understand how it works.

Don't bother coming in for a while, Tumanov had said, the audit will take at least a month! *You are an incompetent and a saboteur! You must be liquidated. Now, go home and wait your turn!* is what he *really* meant I am sure. Tumanov, that clever swine. He was implicated up to his snout and yet he had the sense to marry into the echelons.

Luckily the food situation is taken care of, I have been a wily old bird in my time too, you know. Tins! Tins! Hundreds of them: meat, beans, sausage, jam, jars of pickled cabbage and beets, bags of rice and buckwheat. The concierge leaves a small bottle of vodka by my door once a week for a small advance and I have tea, sugar, and hot water from a samovar. The curtains I keep drawn all the time but at night I can peep through a gap; look out across the Embankment. Winter is nearly done in. If I open the window just a tiny chink I can hear the crack of the ice-flows as they smash into the steel barge under the Bolshoy Bridge. I too must try and be firm! To live each day to its utmost as though it were my last (which, lets face it!) How marvellous to still be drawing breath, breathing the air! If I stick my mouth to the crack I can gulp down big pints of it, feel its chill over my tongue, across my oesophagus and down into my still fully functioning lungs. And yet in my most crimson moments, when the agents of the state are busy and the dreaded footsteps approach (Come on! Come on!) then die away again, I almost long for the coup de grâce. The beatings and the questions, the inevitable confession. But then, terror within terror! Just WHAT to confess? I who have done nothing wrong! Doubt, Comrade! Doubt and lethargy! Old age. Discretion. Standing still. Your silence buys you no friends here, no time. All you warrant is a giant broom to sweep you under the carpet. We have no use for passive acceptance. We are not your grandchildren to be indulged and ignored! This country is ours not yours. No room for Grandad. Get in line!

What a horrific night! The worst I can remember! More arrests. So many flats now standing empty, denuded of citizens. I plucked up the courage (from where?) and glanced down into the courtyard, my nose just over the window ledge. It was the concierge! No more vodka, I immediately, selfishly thought. Poor Nikolai Arsenevich! The old warhorse. I heard the clop of his wooden leg as it plugged through the melting snow. They dragged him to the car and in what kind of a hurry? My God! The terrible fact of that hasty exit stayed with me, kept me up all night, along with the other arrests. Whatever must be done must be done quickly it seems, as though to stop and look at the plates spinning would send them toppling over with a resounding crash. My hour would come. I too would be shuffled off. But where was Nikolai now? I thought, as the dawn nudged through the curtains. Dead or may as well be. I remember his stories of his part in the war, fighting against the Whites, against Kolchak[1] and the rest. Those great running battles (I had seen a few of my own) across unimaginable wastes. The refugees fighting each other like rats, the spittle in a Cossack's beard, the smell of cordite falling like mist after a strafing, the Commissar blinded by shrapnel, directing a charge into a frozen pond. Of course Nikolai had to go, we all have to, I am sure. You can't be sentimental and fussy about the past. Just cut the cord and bury the dead. One glance over our shoulders at 'The Glory Days' will keep us rammed into the mud like elephants! On! On! Our faith must always be with the young, the new breed!

Luckily, I had also contrived to stockpile a hoard of pigment so thank God I have been able to keep working. I ran out of canvas some time ago, so sized up what paper I had and painted on that. Then that too was quickly gone. For the last week I have begun working *alla prima*, straight on to the walls of my room, and I have to admit it's going along tolerably well. The wallpaper is not too absorbent (distempered probably) and I have already finished one wall of my bedroom. I flatter myself that, since I began, I have produced, if not my greatest, then certainly my most consistent body of work in a long time.

As I knew it would be wall-based I hit upon the idea of a frieze, a history, the whole history of the Revolution. The birth of Marx, he and Engels meeting in Paris, Lenin arriving at the Finland Station, Trotsky in his train, heading for the front with the Red Army, Comrade Stalin, Tukhachevsky[2], the whole panoply. You may laugh, but I am quickly running out of red.

That night, the night after Nikolai. No! I mean the morning; my days are the dark hours now. The Footstep

Hours. The Time Of The Banging Door. Anyway, that morning, I dreamt, or rather nightmared up a monster, banging, bulging the glass of the window, a giant invisible monster that became a gigantic wind, and in the dream it felt like the world's end, the blast from a huge bomb. I peeped out (exactly as I would've done in reality, you understand?) and saw the trees along the Embankment, bending almost to the ground, the distant electric sparks from a falling power line fizzed to the floor like a wet firework. My hand rested on the pane and I felt the force of the wind against the glass, pushing me away, dismissing me. In the dream I put on my old army coat and left the room. I walked slowly, with no suggestion of urgency down many flights of stairs, towards the entrance hall. Everyone was still asleep even through the riot of the storm, which made the whole place feel as vulnerable as an upended shoe box. Every window, every door was rattling enough to drop from its hinges. I walked past Nikolai's office and sure enough there he still was, headphones stuck into the wireless, lighting each new cigarette with the final glow of the last. He seemed happy enough even though he was probably dead already (although this paradox never struck home in the dreams midst). Outside - once I had summoned the force to open the rotating door that was barricaded by the wind - the rain was gusting down in every direction at once. The air, rich with river mud was stolen by the wind from right out of my mouth. Thousands of leaves and microscopic bits of twig were whirling around with the rain and the sound was immense. The surface of the pond outside the block was being blown about madly, caught within the maw of its own tiny tempest. I thought of the decorative carp the Housing Committee had placed in there and wondered whether they, or all the fish in all the oceans ever had the slightest inkling of the existence of storms above, beyond their world. A curled-up leaf whipped across the surface like a boat and

I was instantly at its dream-helm; the giant swell propelling me onwards and the carp, like great golden sharks, circling below. Then I was back to my normal size and had to cover my eyes from the needles of rain and the whirling mass of leaves as I stared out past the old apple tree, towards a dark corner of the garden. A large wicker fence had already been blown down and just beyond it, away from all this tempest carnage, I spied the figure of a child and as that mad-dog-wind peaked with an audible moan, we stared at each other across the blasted fence.

It seems that all I ever dream of is wind.

Most of my working hours are filled with, well, with work. I paint constantly, I mean the brush isn't exactly busy from the first smear of colour to the last dip of turps - some moments are required for calculation, for thought, even a little reverie before the brush is plunged back into the fray. Delicately though. Softly. It's not bucket and mop.

Anyway, I try and allow myself regular breaks for rest, food and especially…tea. God keep my samovar safe. It is an expensive one and worth double the money. It is now my dearest colleague, my nurse, my muse all rolled up together. It seems to allow me the right space for contemplation and buoys up my flagging courage. Saint Samovara! Somehow it helps to keep me sane and it's true, my behaviour can sometimes get out of hand. Listening, listening, always listening! Example: I spent two hours last night with my right ear glued to my best ear-friendly wine glass, lying on the floor, probably covering myself in dust now I come to think of it, listening to the passage of events in the flat below. No arrests mark you! Not yet. But judging by the amount of whispering heated, red-in-the-face whispering that was going on down there, well let's just say it won't be long. My consolation (when my knock eventually sounds, my death knell) will be that it is my proper time and my old head will fit that little dimple on the executioner's block as snug as any glove. I have, to some degree, grown into my fate, but there! As soon as I feel a burgeoning sense of peace - that my arrest would cause a happy, joysome tick to jolt across a box at the bottom of a list - this terrible panic is whistling through the keyhole and I am once again fully resolved never to leave the house until they come.

Really, its as though some fragile magic spell lies over the flat and to break the magic, like the snapping of a twig (CLACK!) is as easy as it is impossible.

No, no. Here is where I will be when they want me; I am not such a fool as to rush into the fingerbitten hands of fate. He gets all the breaks, after all. I am stubborn, perhaps even cool-headed enough to make Fate, that fat idiot lose all his puff, break into a sweat, stub every his toe in climbing the stairs on his way to claim me. Even if he is right, fully justified in coming, all well and good. I'm not the one to offer even a glimmer of remonstrance into the face of that old bungler, the old tyrant! But I will not make the whole affair a complete pushover. Why should I? I don't care about the neighbours.

A knock across the way dumped me out of a dream from a great height and the cold sweats were upon me even before I reached the door. I was under the misapprehension that it was the middle of the night when in fact it was not yet midday. I associate the knock on a door and the stomp of a boot with the hours of darkness. Silence for a moment and then the knock repeated (Thanks Be To God) across the hallway. My ear judged Flat 98. I heard the turn of a key. Anyway, show's over, it was the new concierge (Poor Nikolai!) delivering a package. I passed my reflection in the hall. That things should come to this, I pondered. I was nauseous with fear for the rest of the afternoon, could hardly force down that leftover soup.

I was done in. So many nights untroubled by even a whiff of sleep. Every time I began to nod off, I would come to with a start, the remembered jolt of every last knock, rapping along my spine.

I managed finally, sweetfully to sink off around seven for a couple of well-deserved hours. Storms again. Even my dreams refuse to let me alone, buffeting me around like bullies. This time it's my Granny's house on the estuary, the end shack at Dadyanov, reeking of fish guts and engine oil. Outside the tide was surging dramatically. Movement in the foundations. The walls were quivering and the tiles were flying off the roof like flicked cards. I was lying abed, the room was swaying about as though already at sea. Apparently I had no fear of the rising tide? My dream self must have had a child's mind, too young for the awareness of danger. I could tell the wind was just a primer, an emissary for the Great Storm, the feast of wind that was coming straight across the sea, blowing in from the east; the true hurricane that tore through the town like a runaway train.

You might find it strange, but oftentimes, within the eye of my wind-blown dreams, I actually fall asleep. I mean *inside* the dream. Even have a distant awareness of so doing. I think these are my moments of purest, unraddled rest. Think of it. A sleep within a dream. Anyway, suffice to say I slept inside this last one, inside the room, inside the old tumbledown shack at the edge of the estuary inside my head and even those dreams, like an old ship in a shaken bottle, were filled with rattles and cracks.

I could hear Mrs. Zukovsky's dog in the next shack along whimpering and howling in an ever more frantic state. Its kennel (I knew) had caved in and eventually; Mrs. Z had taken him inside. I could tell from the direction of the muffled whines that he was lying under her bed, as indeed I myself had done during a marathon game of hide and seek, played with her boys only a few Sundays before. The same boys, I could now hear through the wall, as petrified as the dog and accompanying his noise with their own duet of sobs and fear-filled moans, which rose and fell in time with the screams of the wind. Finally, in the dream, awaking, I peered out of the window and into the black.

Never a glim of light for miles. I could make out the break of the waves under Granny's window and realised that we were cut off from the land. Wherever father had gone to find us some help, it would be quite impossible to reach us now, leastways not without some kind of boat or raft and the tide was still rising as quick as a thought. I went back to bed, surprised at my own nonchalance. I will float on this bed if needs be, I vowed, suddenly inspired by the ghost of my own courage. I will float along on the tide all the way along to Aunt Alyona's who would have a nice warm fire on the go and there was sure to be toasted cheese, potato cakes and bacon, warm rye bread and sweet tea.

In the dream, my tummy rumbled as I got back into bed, the sea wall seemed to go at just that moment and the house was torn away with a nasty scrape, squealing nails and splintered wood. Everything gave a sudden lurch and the family bible fell from its perch on my shelf, knocking me unconscious.

Now I was granted the role of spectator as the Old Shanty found itself carried away in the dark. What with all the mayhem and destruction the storm was reaping in Dadyanov, nobody but my dream eye even noticed it was gone. Mrs. Z, her old hound and the two boys were too busy drowning. For a while the shanty loomed upright through the flooded part of Dadyanov. Nobody saw it pass but me or ever heard the sound of its tin stovepipe and that old gable end being garrotted by the town's only telegraph wire. Away she went, lugged back into the retreating tide, and soon enough the shivering, besplintered mess was being born along on the remnants of the surge. It did indeed bob down along the bay past Auntie's, unfortunately without stopping and when the *knock-knock-knocking* started it must've been entering the deep ocean, proper. It was an arrest at the end of the hall and went off without a hitch. Quiet as the grave.

Dreams like that were exhausting as any long journey. If it hadn't been for the noise of the arrest returning me to the cold, chickenhearted slab of reality so cruelly, I would've awoken with a sense of renewal, of being revitalised in some way. Of course such feelings soon disappear but are wonderful to behold while they last. In much the same way, during the war, our young eyes would well up with tears at the scent of spring blooms, of piney woodsmoke.

Despite my lack of sleep over the last few days, the paintings continued and, perhaps encouraged by the memory of that last dream, I even went so far as to open the curtains a little wider in the last hours before morning (I hoped nobody would notice) so as to see my palette a little clearer in daylight.

The frieze was changing in accordance with my mood. Now that I had painted the History Of The Revolution (in all its minutiae) in the bedroom and some of the hall, the subject had changed and with it I began to notice the first troubling hints of a new and more personal path. I had started painting my own minor role in the story and I fear that this might have taken the whole thing in a certain direction, striking a much less laudable, more bourgeois and indulgent a note! All of this, all these questionable subjects jostled out of me, despite any argument I might offer with regard to their purpose, the intent of the narrative. It all seemed as though I had vexed myself into an unnatural state of catharsis and the result was this backwardian development. An antithesis I was not even aware of.

For the work was now becoming part of an inner narrative, a personal lifecycle of an extinct dinosaur: my self. Only in hindsight did I realise that profound historical moments; the heroic actions and decisions of the great Soviet leaders had turned into this series of unconnected tableaux about my own history. In my exhausted state of mind, the passages about my involvement in the war had managed, somehow, unbeknownst, to include my birth, my childhood and my early life. How this could've happened made me fearful of the already febrile workings of my brain. Lack of sleep, stress and deprivation of daylight had induced me to fill a yard and a half of wall with imagery, in the middle of some semi-conscious painterly trance. I was about to take a turpsy brush to the whole thing when I was overcome by a sense of epiphany. Deep within me, at my personal earth's core, under many layers of emotional igneous rock, I knew, somehow for sure, that this tiny stretch of painting: self-obsessed, introspective and done without any thought for my usual concerns of structure, for pure form; was far and away the most fascinating and important piece of work I had ever, in my whole long life, mange to produce. I stared at it for hours, even into darkness.

Come what may, I argued against my better nature, I MUST continue to follow this bearing, wherever it leads! So be it! Somehow the path offered an egress, a way out of what felt more and more like a desperate and cruel reality.

My only other neighbour, the General, has gone. As to his character, I can attest that he was certainly possessed of one. He was squat, fat, suitably bald-headed and rubicund, with an under-bite that was quite startling on first acquaintance. Into any room he would carry an ambience of gun oil, sweat and onions. Need one say more? There you have him in a nutshell. Basically everything a Soviet citizen could ask for in a senior soldier! Besides conforming so comfortably to type, he was always good to me. He pestered me so long for a picture of Lenin that eventually I gave him a little pencil study I had done just after the war. Of course he was disappointed. He wanted my version of one of those factory-made paintings you can pick up at the market for a few pennies! Never mind. He was good enough. He and Nikolai used to get drunk once a week in a little place just over the Mokva. Would come back singing all the old songs until the early hours, crying on the stairs in each other's arms.

They came for him last night, I think ostensibly, only to ask questions but changed their minds halfway through the interview, who knows why? Maybe something about the tale told that didn't amuse them, that did not quite hold water enough for them? Anyway, they decided to take him along anyway, what the hell? I heard all this, the whole caper, through my listening glass. Am I going round the twist? For some reason, the whole conversation was spoken in rhyme. But now I come to think of it, this cannot be. Certainly that was how I wrote it down on a scrap of old wallpaper at the time. But that was after several days severe lack of sleep, heard through a concrete wall and with the percussive thump of the hot water pipe as upstairs enjoyed a bath, added to the general ambience. So! Anyway, this is how I set it down.

Interview With The General
I Thought I Heard Through The Wall

(Sounds of muffled laughter)

General: I tell you its true! Why would I lie to you?

Voice #1: It's just that all of us are wondering, how you do it? How high can you build this wall of bullshit?
You knew her history from the outset. Do yourself a favour,

Comrade just admit it! It's all on file, all the cold, hard facts! This is not just recently; this is going way back. Her parents? Wealthy peasants, filthy *kulaks*[3], her brother was a deserter who ended up in the Gulags. She is quite a character, your ex-wife! One in a million! Larger than life! Her dalliances with known traitors! A long list of dubious lovers! Counter revolutionary associations, her subscription to pro-Bukharin[4], Trotskyite publications…blablabla! The list is endless! Tell us, comrade, why so clueless? This is the mother of your family here! You shared the same house, the same bed for five years! And you have the effrontery before us here, today, to deny any knowledge of where her sympathies lay? You knew nothing at all about it, you say! What! No talk of politics at the General's table? A babe in the woods on that subject, eh General?

General: Comrades! Tell me, what have I done? I have been a good Bolshevik since 1921. I haven't seen my ex for over four year. As to what she's done since, I haven't the faintest idea, either what she was up to or who she was seeing, or even whereabouts she was living!
She left Moscow after the divorce and kept custody of the children, of course…

Voice #1: You've been such an obstinate old cuss! I'm running you in. I've had enough. Pavel, help him to gather his stuff!

Voice #2: Come on, comrade! Let's get you dressed!

General: But what have I done to warrant arrest?

Voice #1: Comrade, I'm sure that you can see why anyone, let alone the NKVD[5], might find all this difficult to believe? Your ex-wife, Comrade General? Come on! Please! Do you think even we could be quite so naive?

General: (in earnest) Comrade! I swear! If this is true and Svetlana is guilty of treachery, do me one favour? Tell me where she is! Let me confront her! If she is guilty of what you accuse her, I for one would be more than eager to put the gun to her head and pull the trigger and to the heads of any other traitors! I am not part of this conspiracy! Be assured that all my loyalty lies with Comrade Stalin and the Party! *End of story*!

Another few terrible nights and then, my God! *Tonight*. At first it felt like the rare blessing of silence but that silence grew and grew and was soon so heavy with nothingness that it was nauseating, the instant *before* the punch in the head, spun out for hours, awaiting the inevitable. But the punch never came, only the mounting fear of its arrival. When the footfalls, the door-banging's the hustlings-away don't come, one is left only with the thought of when they will finally re-arrive and such a thought is a hundred times worse. The tension made the walls actually throb. I could feel it. Everyone is terrified - even in their sleep - expecting it. I was bolt upright, never a moment my ear wasn't bolted to the door and the gorge of vomit-fear rising like evaporating bile in my gullet.

I did not sleep at all and I knew I was becoming feverish and angry, I even considered going the whole hog and painting over the History Of The Revolution with black curses or whitewash! Damn them! If they were going to have me destroyed why should I be fool enough to lick the boot that would kick out my lung?

I slept, fitfully for an hour before midday but was still prey to a dream, at first, fraught with the usual monster wind.

See below:

Here I am and here is the storm blowing the sea about like crazy but this time I am below the surface, slowly sinking down to the sea bed. I look up with pleasure at the bottom of the capsized boat, knowing that I need never return. I seem to embrace this new existence blissfully and call to mind the Jules Verne my father had given me. Now I was the *Nautilus*! I could watch with impunity, through the portholes of my eyes as whole phantasmagorias of creatures pass before me, a parade growing in splendour the deeper down I sink. I watch a great shark pass above me, bright flashes from the switchback turns of vast clouds of fish. Huge Portuguese Men O' War float like quippering ghosts and thousands of seahorses prance and rock in the seaweed tops, bobbing up on prehensile tails. As the sea bed looms into sight I see a sunken galleon, bristling with coral cannon, great kelp flags flowing from her fractured masts, treasure and gold doubloons shimmering in the sand where they had spewed out of the ruptured hull. As I land, soft and weightless in the sand, I feel Granny's arm about me, feel myself surrounded by my parents embrace, feel myself return to them safely. Sweet dream!

Breakfast this afternoon was a tin of ham and some boiled potatoes cunningly fried in the pan with a dribble of vodka. I took my fork and mashed it all together. Delicious! And with the memory of my recent sea dream still gladdening my heart, I felt encouraged enough to spend what daylight remained in beginning the central wall of the living room. I decided that my dreams constituted enough of my recent reality to be properly incorporated, be they good or bad. The painting now, the personal slant of it was developing further and further away from the nature of the work in the bedroom (a place where I realise only at this moment, I haven't set foot in almost a week). Now the devil is in the detail. My large bristles and chisel-nosed hogs are lying neglected and my stock of fine-ended squirrels; watercolour sables and sign-writing brushes have been ransacked. The images are becoming ever more miniature in size, rendered quite quickly despite that and yes, somehow or other feel much closer to the painter, to the person I might be, the person I might possibly become were it the case that I should be allowed to live out my days in peace and were not destined to be arrested, tortured and executed at any moment.

I have decided, perhaps under the influence of an incipient constipation, to go back and illustrate the walls of my lavatory with the details of my recent sea dream.

No sign of the General.

Is this a final testament I wonder? If so I should be more specific. I have recorded much on the walls but these images are soon painted over. What if this journal is all of me that is allowed to live? My origins? As I retrace my marks back across the wall I see that almost every event is represented. Here, covering a brown stain of damp is the story of my simple birth. The only people present were my Granny, naturally my mother and at a later moment, my new self. I shot out from between my dear mother's thighs at such a rate of knots that, so the legend went, I would have been an early goner had it not been for Granny's great fat hands, which made a grab at me and managed to arrest my fall by means of my warm, bloody ear. Where was my father when all this was going forward? Well, father was at that very moment having a boil lanced at a hospital some two hundred *versts*[6] away, at Kavan. And though the hospital was nothing much to boast of (a mere twenty beds) it certainly did well by my esteemed parent who suffered nothing in the way of septicaemia, fever of the brain or any ill effects other than the temporary inability to sit in one position for more than a few moments. That our local Doctor, an ex-German known as Kohl should think it necessary for my father to travel all the way through the snow to Kavan, to have a boil on his arse lanced while my mother was left to give birth to me, in a two-room hovel with only Granny and Yevgenia (the dog) for company, defies belief. Be that as it may, this is exactly what befell my poor mother, my Granny and myself and hence the reason Granny had to do the catching with her fat hands and hence the reason why one of my ears has always been noticeably more pronounced than its near neighbour over on the other side. As it was, the whole event was more than poor Yevgenia could stand. She had always been an edgy and fainthearted beast (the sort of dog that caused rabbits to stop in mid-chase, turn around and stare her out of countenance until she sloped away, tail drooping.) My mother's anguished screams, the absence of my father and the general air of panic and impending doom was too much for her ageing dog's heart. When Granny came down to feed the stove, poor Yevgenia (a dog I would come to know by reputation alone) was lying peaceful and quite dead, under the table.

The only reason I mention Yevgenia was the feeling that with her timid soul, somehow, in all the confusion, I had become possessed. From childhood's hour I had always been part-filled with a certain nervousness, an overawing sense of self-awareness, doubt and mortification of mind, convinced that I am some second rate cut price ham, merely acting the part of me and the whole world can see through the paper thin facade of the performance. In point of fact, the only times such feelings have died away have been during five years of war (though that's not saying much, everyone becomes somebody else when they are trying to kill each other), in the secret pages of this journal and when I have been painting. Admittedly, over the years, the more convincing I became at rendering a figure with brush, or ink, the more these sat-upon doubts squeezed their way back out into daylight. All the more reason perhaps, why my latest pictorial adventures, these vain, preening and not wholly unsuccessful forays into selfhood have been so strangely rewarding; briefly unchaining me from the doubt, the extreme self-awareness I seem always to have had. Only yesterday, I had the shock of my life when, turning, suddenly I caught sight of a strange, bearded man in my apartment it was several seconds before I recognised my own reflection, an image that, in all honesty, had utterly freed itself from my memory. Somehow the alchemical fairy who lives within the paint had worked its magic on me and the miniscule detailing of my life, dreams, thoughts and career had produced a merciful forgetfulness of my own image. What a paradox! As though all that was left of me was an eye to see, a hand to hold the brush, all floating in the air. Perhaps it's true that the tale is more than just the teller.

After a none too agreeable dinner of pickled beets and sliced sausage, I slipped into a doze and, quite out of the blue, dreamt I was the Emperor Trajan about to be called back from the Underworld by the chanted prayer of Pope Gregory. At first it was as you would imagine. I was forever running, running desperately stumbling, trampled down and getting up then running again to find a way out of the black caverns of hell. Then thousands of others surrounding me, also trampled down and then born back up, like the foam in a wave. From each passage came the moaning of the damned. Everyone was running as fast as we could, our lungs filled with the smoke of hot coals, close to bursting with the rush. None of us knew from whence we had come or whither we were going, all we knew was this terrible inescapable fear as though we were all of us pursued by some great, slathering, bloodhungry beast that was just at our heels! The tunnels were endless, whichever way we went only took us deeper and deeper into the very marrow of hell and the beast that we knew was nearly upon us was relentless, unstoppable. We never slept or rested our eyes were wept dry with exhaustion, our feet wet with blood and blister and still the panic fear we could never shake propelled us onwards, inexorable. Endlessly along the walls of the caves, down the deepest tunnels we pelted, never stopping. Each one of us, falling again under the pounding feet of the others and still we were born back up again by the terrible tide of souls. My throat had long grown mute from my petrified screams, my ears deaf from the screams of others. There was nothing, not a breath of air, just this constant gaping tortuous agony. Time must have passed and yet not one of us had any notion of its passage. It could be twenty minutes or a thousand lifetimes gone. The pace increased and then suddenly it all fell away, I seemed to be born up and freed from the nightmare and my soul was suddenly soaring through bright, cold air and my lungs filled now with goodness, even though I knew there was hardly anything left of me except for the dust the soldiers were brushing away through the ashes of my ancient tomb and there I was, finally blessed and free and all I had left to thank Him was a parched and withered old pagan tongue, but that seemed to be enough.

I awoke with new feeling of optimism and even though it only lasted until fully blotted out by the day: some real courage.

The next night, back to normal and I was woken by the most terrible noise! An arrest, a workingman, (an engineer, I think, on the new Moscow/Volga canal) and he positively refused to go without putting up one hell of a fight! Lord how I admired him and how clearly did I envisage my own forthcoming arrest, which would play out like nearly all the others, the opposite of this: footsteps, a sharp rap on the door, a *Yes, comrade?* followed by a *please come with us, comrade!* and then a final *of course, comrade!* More (very polite) footsteps down the stairs and into the waiting black car and then, lickety-split towards oblivion. But here, now, the engineer refuses to listen to reason. Hasn't the good manners to go out with a whimper. It appears he hasn't done a thing wrong and refuses to leave his wife (Natalya) who is ailing, whom he cannot leave on her own God knows! If they wanted to talk well, talk! He wasn't stopping them. They could ask him anything, he was an innocent as a child as anyone would tell you, he was a shock worker, a one hundred per cent red steel Bolshevik! If they wanted an interview they could do it there and then while they were all nice and cosy and where he could get up now and then to make Natalya a cup of camomile tea if she wanted one! Look at her! Just look at her, he demanded, the poor thing is worn out! A martyr to that kidney! If he left her alone now who would bring her hot soup every evening when she could hardly stand? Proceedings carried on like this for a good hour and a half. Eventually a superior was called in. I took a bold peep through the keyhole (there was so much noise I was sure they wouldn't notice) I saw the officer arrive, uniformed and unshaven. A big man: a little jowly, a touch green about the gills. Well, things soon shifted up a gear. Three minutes, I counted before the engineer was being carried unconscious down past the stairwell, with blood pouring from his ear. What is more they bought his wife along for good measure, still in her invalid's chair! What could she have done to hurt them I ask you? She hadn't left that flat in upwards of a year according to Old Nikolai. Anyway, far be it from me to stick my nose in but the whole affair left an even more bitter taste in my mouth than usual. I suppose someone can be as guilty as Judas without ever having once doubted the cause. They stand accused who stand in the way of progress. Twenty years ago such people were firing guns at me, so why pity them now? But can they all be saboteurs?

The next evening I was trying to utilise the last of what light there was to finish part of the main wall, when I found myself beginning to paint a story my mother had told me as a child. I think she always told it to make me feel more at home in my shell. I had forgotten it until that moment and shall try and tell it here, by your leave, to refresh my memory. This is how my mother would tell it and she always had a brisk, matter of fact way of peeling open a story.

The Tale of the Silent Kid

Well, I'll tell you. Right up until the very moment he stopped speaking, the kid had been a famous chatterbox. Lord above, yes! His poor family were oftentimes driven half bananas by his constant yappering!

Anyway, the events I am about to relate happened quite suddenly, inexplicably in the middle of a geography lesson.

The kid was eight years old and because of his slack-jawed jabbering in class, the teacher had put the kid's desk right up next to his so that the kid was within easy reach of a cuff about the head or a good tweaking of the ear should he begin to grow restless and start off with his infernal gob. Of course Ancient Rome would usually be a subject confined to the history lesson but the teacher, Professor Chernekov had, only that morning, happened upon an article pertaining to that very period in the local rag and was giving forth on a subject (to wit: the eruption of Vesuvius) that happened to be a pet one for him. He had after all crammed almost all the Latin Grammar he had from an edition of the letters of Pliny the Younger, an ancient Roman scholar present at the aforementioned cataclysm and the study of volcanoes, a fundamental part of geology did in fact fall into under his geographical remit.

So, to cut straight to the chase, our Professor Chernekov was giving a full description of the environs of the Bay of Naples, of Vesuvius, of Pompeii and Herculaneum when our hero, the chinwagger stuck out his paw to ask a question regarding what exactly had happened when Vesuvius had exploded? Dear Professor Chernekov took the question in the proper (geological!) spirit and proceeded to outline for the kid and for the whole class the catastrophic events following the explosion: the huge column of smoke and debris, the falling rocks, the gush of the lava streams. He talked about the destruction of Pompeii, the asphyxiation from the massed clouds of poisonous fumes, the white plastered bodies of survivors, cast from the holes they left in space: a sleeping mother and child, a dog.

That was when whatever had clicked inside the kid's head had clicked and this total, this utter non- communication had begun.

And it wasn't as if the kid had just lost the spoken part of language. No. He was struck so dumb on every front that he would not or could not make even the vaguest sign, no, not even a nod of approval, a barely perceptible shake of the head, a slight widening of an eye. And yet apart from the not speaking, the kid continued on just as before, only without the vaguest attempt to converse with anybody. At all.

His Mother and Father were, at first, nearly as dumbfounded as he was. When finally, they did begin to give voice, the fact that his state could not in any way be accounted for by the Teacher or the Doctor led to immediate accusations of playacting and the constant approach of a sound beating, from either one or the other (or both) all of which caused the kid to not react in exactly the same way. He was soon put into the hands of a local faith healer and herbalist. What else could they do? The healer diagnosed a form of catatonia. Well it was either that or sleeping sickness. Back at home; the kid spent most of his time with his head at an odd angle, looking out of the window and down onto the village square. His toys lay neglected. When he wasn't a permanent fixture at the window, his head would be on the pillow (at that same funny angle!) and he would be deep asleep. He would sleep and sleep. He slept so often through his lessons that unless he snored, the teacher as well as all his classmates, soon learned to ignore it and let him nod off in his own sweet way. Mother and Father could not for the life of them, get him out of bed for breakfast and when they shouted slapped and kicked, even resorting to reason once or twice, well, nothing. None of it registered. Sleeping sickness! Let him lie! Saith the healer, whose star was definitely no longer in the ascendency. But you know those famous sleeping jags never seemed to affect his studies, unless there was something to read out to the class he managed pretty well. Certainly when he had been a thoroughgoing blabberhound the patience of the good Professor was tested to the extreme. Now though, all was well and tranquil with the class and let me ask you which teacher in the whole history of education has ever objected to such a state of affairs? That he was getting better and better at school was a real glimmer of hope for his troubled parents. Naturally, he was beaten and bullied for a short time by some bigger boys, some village toughs but they soon gave up the ghost; he was so uninvolved and indifferent it became too much of a one-sided affair for those young gentleman, something of a chore. Pretty soon life began to get back to normal.

But, hold on! We are only just getting started! Soon enough, another change began to come over the kid, much to the renewed disappointment of his, by then, almost resolved-to-it parents. Although this new development was much more gradual it was, if anything even a trifle more worrying than the last, because this time it constituted a definite physical change! Simply put: his left ear began to grow at a faster rate than his right. Significantly faster. Noticeably faster. Not only that, it began to discolour. First it became much paler than its opposite number, then a sickly pallid green, then much redder, now a dim orange colour, then it proceeded to bloom in a fortnight from a light shade of ochre to an increasingly angry yellow and then, finally and it seemed, permanently…GOLD! All the time, through every rainbow shade the ear had continued to grow in size and once again, the kid's parents were left quite helpless in the face of this new aberration. There was nothing to be done in the way of stopping it. The poor father was nearing the very outskirts of madness and when they were told by the flummoxed Doctor that nothing more could be done, not even (their first choice) amputation, the kid's poor Mother let out a scream that nearly parted the Doctor's hair!

Meanwhile, any previous problem with communication was, by this time, more or less taken for granted. Regular visits to the healer had yielded up little more than the result of three enemas and the fact that the kid was of unusual intelligence for a boy of this region and there was no reason why he should've stopped speaking the way he had. He (the healer) advocated honey tea and as many dealings with other children as could be contrived. Perhaps, had they followed this sage advice something might have been done in the language department but the bare truth is that the kid's parents were rapidly losing interest in the speech problem as, by then, the boy's ear had already grown to the same size as his head

And what exactly was going on inside that head you might wonder? What was his opinion on all the recent changes so miraculously worked upon him? Well, perhaps it would surprise you to learn that he was as completely unmoved by his massive ear growth as he had previously been by his unaccountably sudden loss of speech. Remarkable, eh? Mind you, it was not as though he was cold-hearted child, far from it! You have already heard tell of his logorrhoea. He was just, in point of fact, elsewhere. As soon as he got home after school, the evening always followed the same course, with little deviation, much to the muted fury of his parents!

1. Supper. To be eaten (of course) without comment but never complaint, in fact mostly with some gusto.

2. Homework. As above.

3. The window is opened and the kid rests his chin on the frame, tilts his head at an angle unusual enough to have been already twice commented upon.

4. He jumps into bed and falls into sleep as though from a great height!

Of course what we now know, with the benefit of hindsight is that the kid, with his new ear, his golden ear could hear EVERYTHING. Every. Single. Thing. And it truly astounded him.

The speech, we know, had long since gone. Blown up along with Vesuvius, suffocated from his mouth and encased in pumice like the good citizens of Pompeii; otherwise what he could hear would have left him just a speechless.

He felt like a conduit, his whole body like a huge golden funnel for all the sounds in the world to be poured into! Somehow the ear managed to control its own reception of sounds, to grade, classify and manage them as though possessed of a magical valve. Human speech in any form was delightful and he found he was soon able to distinguish from each particular timbre, a whole host of implications: secret depths of meaning and character. He never mourned his own death of speech, the silencing of his own vocal chords and why should he indeed? How much more wonderful to listen than to speak! At the river he stood on the shore and trained the ear onto the roll of the current, hearing it as though for the first time. He felt he could distinguish the strength and velocity of every separate ripple as it lapped towards him. To hear such sounds: the secret sounds of the earth, was the kid's great unending joy. Animals amazed him! When a blackbird sang he could distinguish its mate over the hill as well as the answering chirrups of their offspring – the fledgling, there under the hedge, at the edge of the cemetery. He heard the nightingale's tongue quiver against its beak. At the estuary, where he loved to sit, he heard the ululations of a porpoise, out in the deep-water channel. He could hear the air move across his arm, the squeak of a goose bump as it stood up against the cold.

As the kid grew, so did his incredible listening power, until, soon enough, the valve began of itself to close off access to mere earthly sounds and the kid gradually began to hear the unfamiliar sounds of the universe itself. The distant roar of the sun, the nasal whine of a passing meteor, the twinkling resonance of a star and finally, the strangest sound he had ever heard: the low bass boom that still resounded off all the planets, the echo of the fist great sound, the creation of the earth.

It's all gone on to the wall now. Every part. There is something about stories like this that keep me from my fear not only in speaking but in painting and I wish I knew what it was. When I paint them, BOO! Away go those terrible panicky fears of fates steamroller. Should pictures tell stories? Is it just illustration? What would Malevich[7] say? The Suprematists would laugh in my face and at the other extreme, my old Socialist Realist comrades would kick my arse down the stairs. Caught between two stools! And yet I can see old Malevich a little clearer now. A friend at the Artists Union let me see some of those paintings of his that had been confiscated. I was shocked at the time, now I think I understand a little more. Even though I seem to be travelling on the other side of the road, wherever he is, a blessing on him and…Golden Strokes!

Anyway painting was always going to be suspect if it didn't involve the industrial worker, the proletariat. If it told peasant stories or was just a set of abstract shapes, what else but a conversation piece? Bourgeois apartment fillers! Maybe painting itself is a redundancy in light of photography or most vitally: the cinema - a more fugitive medium, whose pace and movement and mass appeal can keep up with the people, the struggle upward into the light!

Despite all that, it is true that my painting has been my staff and comfort; this noting down of thought into image has helped me immensely here. And now, when I step back and look at all the work I have already done in just a few weeks, there is a great feeling, perhaps again of dubious bourgeois origins, but nonetheless as sweet on my senses as honeysuckle. A feeling of pride, of probably momentary elation felt in a job well attempted and if it is never to be finished then so be it! Well, nobody can ever take what I have tried to achieve away even if they painted over it tomorrow!

Four sudden knocks at the door this morning had me

straight back in the groove of fear, of sweat-filled panic. I waited, as still as a stone behind the door I had been touching-up, my brush poised in mid-air. Give or take ninety seconds between each set, three sets of four quick raps, rat-ta-tat-*TAT!* No, not the knock of a group of men, just a single hand, nonetheless certainly a nasty wake-up call from death. As whoever it was, was walking calmly away I, like a fool, was too precipitate to see the back of who it might be and I happened to tread (oh, *thank* you!) on the only floorboard in the whole house that creaks. The figure stopped for ten, fifteen seconds…and then carried on towards the stairs. I got a sighting of him at just the last moment. The new concierge, no less! Yes, this will mean only trouble, a first tremor before the earthquake, a shot across my bows. He would be sure to report something suspicious to the next officer to cross his path and I would be down those stairs and into the back of a Black Mariah quicker than a mouse's fart. Nowadays, everyone is a nosey parker watching everybody else's every move. All of us, heading for the pyre and the fellow in front of you is telling anyone who will listen how your flesh will almost certainly burn quicker than his so, by rights, you should go first, not him. Time is a factor, the fat from the burning bodies might put out the fire, and then the sudden cry: everybody can go home, all done for today! Such bestial scrabbling for an apple core of life! Thanks but no thanks. I am getting off this nasty little merry-go-round, jumping off before the shit hits the wall. Perhaps I should go ahead and turn myself in? Frogmarch myself down to the Lubyanka[8], throw myself into a cell. Wake myself up in the middle of the night, have myself tortured, beat the soles of my own feet with a rubber truncheon! Then, when I have heard my own confession take myself down to the basement and shoot myself in the back of the neck. At least it will save on man-hours; these fellows at internal security must be getting hardly a wink of sleep. The call should go out!

"Every Soviet Citizen who believes himself guilty of treason or sabotage (in thought or deed) should save us the bother and try themselves at home. Free self-torture and execution kits are to be made available for every self-implicated enemy of the people!"

When though, when will they come? It has been so long I am starting to have these long moments of reprieve when the thought of my imminent demise drifts away and I am left in the middle of a holiday of thoughts and, to be honest, it slows me right down. I end up mooning about the place, letting my tea grow cold, just painting, staring out of the curtains instead, at the sky and at the river. Then the realisation hits you and you see clearly again, a clarity made a thousand times more terrifying when remembered in parallel with these tender moments of reverie, of amnesia. Just because those stolen moments have such sweetness to them, every time they come feels like the last. The thing is that, in these moments, I am simply being. I am being allowed to be and when I crash back down to earth it is with the sudden awareness that it must be my fate to NOT be, very soon. Oh, how horrible.

I am resolved to carry on with the painting no matter what occurs. Therefore, on a whim, I have, moved what pieces of furniture I possess into the bedroom and taken up the whole carpet so I can utilise the floor as well as the ceiling in my search for space for frieze space. After a clean, the parquet came up nicely. Luckily it has been a long time gone since its last varnish, so it would take the paint quite well enough for my purposes, after a few coats of old primer. I spent the day on that and left it overnight to dry.

Morning. The day comes down on Moscow like a migraine and this building, this huge creamy white house of party-cards rears up into the day like a broken snout, a spare joint jutting out from a broken limb. At times it is as

...d as any monolith, an obelisk in the sand. It's only in summer's doldrums that it starts to become almost sentient, a breathing mass like the pitted cells of a lung. An entity, in and of itself. Old Nikolai called it The Great Angler, catching the ambitious party member who comes up for air at the top, who is then scooped up into the net, gobbled up and then vomited, shat out into the death cell basements and the Gulags. Once, last summer, Nikolai took me down to the boiler room to find a spare key; the steel doors were open and those great boilers roared and gurgled as we passed, the tortured heart of the place, malevolent somehow, and luciferous. Since the arrests began the burps and gurgles of the heating have had ever more malign implications. Blocked arteries, overheated varicose veins, the whole place smells of boiled blood when you turn on the hot tap. They say it's the rust, the iron. In my weaker moments I begin to think that all the evil here present is powered by its hot coal furnace.

Makes me think of my own body which is even more done in than the plumbing. After all its been in and out of more scrapes than I care to mention. Only just now I was standing naked looking at it in the half-length wall mirror. I've more dents and scars than an old pit pony someone's lobbed on top of a slag pile. I will take you on a brief tour and I think it might prove informative to the student of geography. Sure enough, the closer one looks, the more it resembles Russia herself. There might not be much left of the Urals but there is an ample supply of steppe. Lets start chronologically: the larger ear I have already alluded to, bent at the top fold, like a naughty dog's. Peeping through the burnt forest of beard, at the centre of my cheek is a small, crescent-shaped scar where I was hoofed by a goat, aged three. Over my right eye is a just discernible nick: I was swimming in a lake and some other boys tried to hold me under water for too long. I panicked and when I got to the surface, I knocked my head against the raft. The left canine was chipped by Czech shrapnel during the fall of Yekaterinburg, on the day after they killed the Tsar[9]. At the top of my upper left arm: the ghost of a scar from a shabbily lanced boil (I suffer from my poor father's complaint) and on my last left rib is the scar from a Cossack's sabre, had on a march for bread, just before the Revolution. Only twenty years ago and it feels like a hundred! I was actually running away (just as I was at Yekaterinburg! But then so were we all!) trying to shake off a different Cossack who didn't like the look of me. I was legging it down an alley off the Arbat[10] and as I got to the end, another great shaggy brute was waiting, blade glinting. As it turned out, I had to call so sudden a halt that I skidded under his horse and felt the swish of his sword above my head. I was just rolling out the other side when he must've leant down in his stirrups and poniarded me under my arm as I went by, the bastard. Luckily his great charger didn't bat an eyelid or I would've been trampled as well for my pains. I dined out on that beauty for weeks afterward! At the top of my thigh I have the mark of a bayonet thrust that nearly killed me at Barguzin, on my last day of war. Thanks to that and to my earlier encounter with the Cossack, my name got about in the right circles and when the last corner of the old Russia finally began to crumble (as all rotten-arsed, jerry-built structures must) and the war finally finished, I ended up with a plum job designing sets at the Meyerhold Theatre[11]. What a character he was, the Great Meyerhold! The human inferno! I have never seen so much energy. He came through those famous double doors like The Bandit King, his great konk cutting a dash through the air! Now they say he is a spent force, a Symbolist reactionary and I must say I find all that difficult to believe.

Today is my birthday. I am dropping off for fifty winks. One for every year I have been alive!

The dream comes. A hot wind like the real world and a black mist of storm, this time inside what was my room and has now become a cellar wherein some dead figures lie broken against the wall, all pistol shot. I recognize the Tsar's Van Dyke moustache and beard and I must be his son. My friends from the Meyerhold, Masha and Pyotr, now my killers, shoot and shoot but cannot seem to hit me even though I hear their bullets thwack into the damp wainscotting behind my head. I start to cry and the room is instantly drenched in a rainstorm of my tears, cascading down the walls. I lie down on a mattress in the corner and the storm worsens, I have to roll myself in the blankets to keep them from flying away. My ears pop with the thunder cracks. I wake up feeling ready to puke, as though I had just stepped off a fairground ride.

Yes. It is true, I admit it. Physically, I am in a sorry state nowadays. When I come to think of it, the very minute I passed thirty-five the whole weight of gravity seemed to fall upon my head. Suddenly I could hardly stretch a canvas without a week of muscle pain, cramp. My arches began giving me gyp. My hair started the sound the retreat on top around then too, fingers started to ache from too much painting after only a couple of hours. All in all I have become a sack of shit to behold and the last few weeks haven't helped much either. Not just my nerves but also no greens for days, no vodka, remember? Only tinned food and no daylight to speak of. Here I am in the mirror again and my face seems to be disappearing into the wall. I look like a bearded shroud. Christ at Emmaus. Split-lipped, pallid as a ghost and eyes like two fried eggs in a bucket of blood.

This morning a letter was placed under my door, in fact, maddeningly, only half-posted (cunning?). Half a corner remained on the other side so that if I took it in, whoever posted would know the flat was totally occupied.

They needn't think I am no match for them! With a pencil, I drew a faint mark where the letter aligned with the inside of the door. I waited until the last hours of night, quickly drew it in, opened, read it (luckily unsealed), and replaced it accurately. The letter was to inform me that next Friday (a week) the new electric fire alarm system would be tested for the first time and every occupant was ordered to assemble at the bottom of the building by the fishpond. Every apartment was to be left open and unlocked as part of the procedure so that the resident fire officer and the concierge could check every inhabitant was evacuated.

So, my time was up. Whether this was a ruse to flush me out or simply the workings of coincidence, I knew that I must either leave the flat and present myself for the roll call, or be discovered during the search. Serious questions would then need to be asked about this apparent hermit and, of course the fantastical state of the state-owned walls. This was a another wake-up call. Zero hour. I have to act. Must think of a plan to gain me some way out of the clutches of that old killerbear Fate (whose bloody paw marks were all over this latest twist). I needed some more time to think, or rather NOT to think, to think about nothing at all so as to allow the solution to breath itself into the world by osmosis, to reproduce without any interference. Like an aphid.

After the last of the last tin of peaches and a mouthful of sausage, I began to paint. Thoughts of my time, my wonderful time at the Meyerhold came rolling in like waves and soon I was up to my knees in not thinking.

It was while I was there that I met Pyotr and dear Masha who I have mentioned. Pyotr was like me, a painter of scenes and maker of scenery, his own speciality: the background landscape, an area of expertise he hardly ever had cause to put to much use at the Meyerhold. We had trained at the same school after the war. Pyotr had been invalided out in

'21 after losing three toes to the cold in Mongolia fighting that mad bandit, Ungern von Sternberg[12].

At the Meyerhold we had both fallen straight away for the same actress: Masha Stepanova, me in my quiet, nervous way, he (being a true Caucasian) offering his allegiance to the very depths of his soul, swearing he would move the Five Finger Mountain[13] to hold her pretty dimpled chin betwixt his fingers! But what a woman she was! It breaks my heart to even think of her. The sort of woman to take a young man's breath away. Full of joy! Her smile would part the oceans! Oh, God. I cannot speak of it.

Eventually we all got to be on friendly terms. She came from my part of town. I even took her out for tea one afternoon and for days was flushed like a ninny with the novelty of my success!

Clouds soon darkened over the sun. I realised it was not I but handsome Pyotr she cared for and I am sure, what woman could help but fall into those alpine pools he had for eyes? I realised I was just in the way. I knew they both cared for me of course but couldn't stand it. I left the company with a blackened heart and never saw either of them again.

I heard the cleaners late this morning talking as they polished the parquet. Here is a rough transcript:

The Conversation of the Cleaners

Cleaner #1: ...they say this Comrade Yezhov[14] is almost a dwarf!

Cleaner #2: That at least is true. My Pavel saw him at a rally and reported back that he hardly came up to Kaganovitch's[15] belt buckles. All you could see over the top of the podium was his cap.

Cleaner #1: They say he is behind…*(inaudible whisper)* …and as well as that, all this latest nasty badness.

Cleaner #2: Then why doesn't Stalin kick his bum for him, that's what I want to know? Pavel says that even the police are running out of police! They sweep out all the baddies and now there is nobody left to mind the baby!

Cleaner #1: What baby? Anyhow, you talk too much!

Cleaner #2: I am a good citizen. Lots of people are beginning to wonder.

Cleaner #1: There is an old Ukrainian proverb…

Cleaner #2: Where do you find them all? Anyway, I thought you were a Kazak?

Cleaner #1: "Eyes and ears open, mouth shut!"

Cleaner #2: So, apparently even old Nikolai was an agitator! A saboteur!

Cleaner #1: Stop, stop! My head hurts with all this! If they say he was bad, he was bad. Look at the rest of them! I read in the paper that even Bukharin was working for the enemy, the swine!

Cleaner #2: I know better!

Cleaner #1: Well you had better stop your gob and do your job or someone will clean the floor with you! What do you think? *There is a shortage of mop pushers now?*

I remember, a few months earlier there had been an incident outside in the corridor. Some loathsome pig of a child (I sound like an ogre but it really *was* loathsome, I had had run-ins with this one before!) had started playing out there: a good hour cycling up and down on a knackered old tricycle while his mother busied herself with doing whatever it is such mothers do (knocking back a swift one or trying her head for size in her new oven). Inevitably the brat had taken a header down the stairs and of course there was no sign of Mama. What else could I do but try and help? I mean no matter how downright annoying it was, we have a duty to our fellow citizens. So, like a rat out of a drainpipe, away I went, pelting out of the flat and down the hall to save the child. Well he certainly was out cold, the piss-ant, lying all akimbo on the first floor landing, in what the murder reports always used to call a crumpled heap. Well there I am at the top step all geared and ready to run down, staunch the flow, feel for broken bones and all that, when a big fat hand pushes me aside and there she is, the mother! careering down the steps after her little Benny who, incidentally has just come round and is screaming-up a storm, enough to summon back the legions of the dead. Suddenly Mummy fixes her rat's ass eye on me! Why are you standing there you brute? He could've died! I began stammering out an explanation when I realised she had already sprung to the conclusion that young Benny had not fallen but been pushed, pushed by the hand of the vicious childslayer stuttering like a bearded madman above her. When the penny dropped, I had no choice but to turn around 180 degrees and stomp back to my room, slamming the door a shade to hard.

Well, little wonder that few of the neighbours bothered much with me after that! Not that any of them have ever been around for long! Little Benny's boggle-eyed Dad, who had come down later to half-heartedly demand an explanation was just a stenographer, a pen pusher at Internal Affairs.

Nevertheless, Nikolai told me confidentially that Little Benny is now tricycling around an orphanage in Siberia.

I am quickly working my way across the parquet. I had applied the wall paint as a primer, and drew out some squares, the lines of the parquet assisting my progress in this, quite handsomely. I have managed to achieve more and more of a trance-like state whereby I hardly know *how*, let alone *what* I am painting. But progress has been good, even my lack of red paint has hardly hindered me. I have thrown down figures and events willy-nilly and, over the next days, by the time I began to near the opposite wall, even I myself, as a subject matter seemed to have slunk away from the painting, although I was only half aware of it. Truly the whole thing was now following a course of its own, only the process of making and of finishing seemed relevant now, the narrative, the story felt like it had been taken out of my hands. Not that I was guided by spirits but to stop to consider anything seemed pointless when it had all flowed so well. I had left a narrow walkway free from paint that led back to the kitchen, so I could occasionally return there for what nourishment remained: buckwheat porridge and the last of my tea. Having got right into the corner I found myself fairly stymied by the presence of the radiator. I turned off the water supply in the hall, hunted down a spanner and unscrewed it from the wall. I found as I lifted the whole thing free I was confronted by a beam of light coming through the rusty wadding. It turned out that, instead of concrete, there was nothing more than a thin panel separating my living room from the flat next door. The flat having been unoccupied for a while (and for the usual reason) I decided to investigate. What, after all did I have to lose at this stage? I began to make more room around the hole, picking at the old plaster with my big palette knife. Eventually I pushed through the panel, only half papered over and lying behind what I could now see was a large, chenille covered sofa and as I pushed and scrambled my way through the tiny gap into the flat it felt like the beginning of an adventure whose borders were limitless. Indeed, it occurred to me that I could keep going throughout the entire floor as soon as each family was evicted and move on before their replacements arrived! Digging my way through, taking up the leftovers of each life, each defunct existence until the new one appeared in its stead. Living out my life as the inhabitant of voided spaces, like a dung beetle.

But I was getting ahead of myself. As it was, this place seemed promising. My ex-neighbours had been a quiet and tidy couple in their late thirties He an unsuccessful playwright, she a teacher. Childless. I found I couldn't even remember their names. Nikolai (the voice of doom!) had told me the writer, had 'disappeared' and not long after that, she had been found floating face down by the coal barges. Poor bastards. They had certainly left a lot behind; whoever had left last (him or her?) had swept the floor and put the broom and dustpan just by the door. Boxes had been piled up in the hall but not yet claimed by any of their family. I looked inside the top one, mostly papers and at the bottom: in soft folds of tissue: a small collection of clockwork toys and automata (him?) The kitchen was identical to my own. I began rooting around like Crusoe in the shipwreck, for biscuits and flintlocks before she smashes against the rocks. There was a generous stash of tins, some dried pulses and rice in the larder as well as (God rain down blessings on their memory! Illuminate their graves with sunlight!) a small, unbroached packet of tea. Three wasps lay dead in a perfect line under the kitchen window, an audience to the late history. Would their stings still function, I wondered? Fingering each of their desiccated thoraxes, I found that they didn't. I opened the window two fingers, and blew them off the ledge. I would've liked to see how long it took them to drop.

That night I moved all my materials as well as my samovar into the empty flat next door. I slept well and dreamlessly which only added to my conviction that the magic spell had been left behind with the paintings, in the old flat. Next morning, I knew that dreaded fire alarm would sound. I thought it best to conceal myself as best I could, behind the large sofa when the inspection began.

Thoughts of Masha and Pyotr. I admit to having been less than honest. It is a fact that I may have been implicated, that I was involved in…that I was inadvertently…that it was through my…but he that would lie to his own journal, what kind of man is he? I admit that I was too cowardly to own even to myself what it was I did. When I sit and contemplate the small piece of painting about that part of my life, out in the hall, the events are indistinct, the colours: dark indeed. The way I behaved has made them difficult days to revisit, to even think about, for me it was, though filled with what I thought were the best intentions, me it was who betrayed my two dear friends. Me it was who caused their downfall.

I was a different person then. We have to acknowledge that at the outset. Their relationship became to me an act of the most terrible treason, It may be that I felt an act of retribution would bring them to a reawakening, a sudden volte-face. The final development, how it all came about was, in the end, via a denouncement, made in confidence and with the assurance of total anonymity from the Party representative at the theatre. In all honesty I felt that Pyotr's constant complaints, his diatribes against the actions of the State had gone far enough. I warned him of that, man to man. He of course would not listen to me, why should he? Who was I to him? I felt as though this constant anti-Soviet railing was part of some illness, a febrile convulsion that was contagious enough to attack the weak-minded, and the impressionable. I was concerned less the contagion spread and begin to affect Masha as well. So, in hoping that she at least, could be caught in time, literally pulled back from what I then would of considered a personal disaster: sedition, possible treason against the State, I gave her name along with his. After being closely observed for two weeks by NKVD operatives, they were both arrested. Like a fool she refused to denounce him. They ended up in the punishment system out East, being rehabilitated like the rest, and I never heard from them, again.

What I did, I can remember feeling, yes, it has to be done. It is the right, the only thing to do. Yet somehow I felt I should've been involved more. I was never consulted by the Party. The outcome was too extreme, not what I had meant to happen. All this is a part of my life I find it difficult to discuss. Even here and only to myself, to these pages.

Once I was told (Nikolai again?) just how many bees buzz about this great hive of Little Russia, this citadel by the river. How many thousands? Waiters for the restaurant, laundrywomen, electricians, cleaners, teachers for the school and staff for the telegraph office and the gymnasium, doctors, projectionists, hairdressers for the salon, plumbers and carpenters, shop workers and window cleaners, kindergarteneers, mechanics for the garage. A fizzing white brain, a city within a city. Even the architect who designed it lives in a flat up on the 13th. The occupants come and go. Mostly now, they just go. Rooms stand idle (the one I am writing from) and the Party faithful, even though they are getting younger, are beginning to hear the rumours regarding the presence of The Dark Stranger behind every painted number: Death feeds here. You can smell it, and a flat on one of these countless hallways is a venom-baked blessing. Take a wrong turn at the end of the hall and, like Alice falling down the rabbit-hole, you could end up in the

Lubyanka. Even if you already work there. Especially if you do.

Flying this time. Pulled off the earth by great rolling vortex of wind, a tornado and then pulled up into the front of a great storm. Carried at great speed across a fierce blue sky. No feelings of elation though, only the horror of the knowledge, the slackening of the wind, the soon-to-come fall. Then, an apex reached, down I was going, my breath dead in my mouth, careering towards a green tropical sea. I smash down into it and am immediately disintegrated, broken into pieces. A seagull flies off with my still seeing eye, a turtle with my hearing ear.

The Fire alarm! They came this morning! Christ! Nearly had me going in my pants, even though I knew it was coming, in fact was all I had been thinking about since the last bit of painting. (Those last passages of painting elude me now: weird marks and semi-figures, almost hieroglyphic?) I leapt down the back of the sofa and proceeded to panic. Started shaking, shaking. Ten minutes later the keys were shaking in the door of my old flat. I heard the expected exclamations of surprise (the painting!) my name was called. Moments later, when I heard that door slam; I quickly whipped back into the old space through the partition. I heard the concierge take a look inside the new flat (he would've known it was empty) then *that* door slammed and I hightailed it back through again, dragging the radiator into place behind me. The alarm rang for five, ten more minutes and then silence. How strange a silence for me, filled as is was with my own disappearance, a form of death even. I looked around me with new eyes. This flat is totally white. No pictures on the walls. No fittings to speak of, only a tap in the kitchen and a stove. A blank canvas. As soon as things quieted down I would try to begin some new painting. No more oil paint left but enough pigment and Gum Arabic for some rudimentary watercolour. I must try and make a fresh start. I admit I have been brought fairly low by my new situation. It felt at first as though, with this weird rebirth into the new flat, I might be allowed a new lease of life and the paintings could begin again. As it is I have a vague notion that something of me has been amputated, something that is still left in that room.

I heard the new concierge and some other man in there only this morning. They were discussing my disappearance and what to do about it. Who to tell? It appears as I have flung them into a bit of a pickle. Nobody wants to call the attention of the proper authorities to my loss, said the other man, just in case we are the ones called to account for it. To name it, he said, would be to bring it into the air and in a sense lay claim to it. Well then, what would you advise? asked the younger man, the new concierge. To keep a lid on it comrade, he answered, at least for another week or two. I have a contact, he said, who tells me the shit is in constant flight at headquarters! Everyone is accusing everyone else of letting it fly or trying to make their neighbour hold the buckets. Heads roll. They say (he said), that even the Commissar General is under suspicion and there are any number of problems in the organisation. The last thing they will want to know about is some maniac of a wall-dauber who has painted himself all the way up his own arse and then jumped down the hole. For now, tell no-one, the voice said, and I promise I will do the same until we meet again in a week. And what about the paintings on all these walls? asked the concierge, should I get the decorators to clean it up? No, leave it. Await developments. My feeling is he has been 'taken in' and forgotten about. It has happened before. Nobody told us about the industrial designer on the eighth who had been removed. It was only when the trial started that we found all that out. Of course that was before your time. Wait two weeks, like I say comrade. If he hasn't turned up by then we will start proceedings. Until then, *schtum*!

Understood? Yes it was understood. So. Two weeks. And then what? How long before everything started to blow over and the flats would begin to be reoccupied? What would I do when the food ran out? I had to utilise my time. I resolved to begin painting the following day.

That afternoon, when I was having a look through all the boxes and trunks, I came across what looked like a diary that must have been overlooked during the search of the flat. In fact it was a story and the more I delved into it, the more interested I became. Who had written it I had no clue but it is of some peculiar interest. In case all their belongings are gathered and thrown away, I enclose a transcript on the pages below.

The Story I Found In A Trunk

When I came to it was from being shaken awake by the wild-eyed purser who himself quickly vanished. What happened to that purser, I never discovered. The boat smelt of panic, cordite and bile. I knew she was sinking. Even down under two decks the noise of the wind and the sea was tremendous. I bumped my way out into the gangways and up the nearest ladder. There was not a man to be seen. As I climbed I sensed no forward movement and realised the engines had stopped. Seconds later I was at the bridge. The number one pushed past me sluggishly, white of face and without a word. They were abandoning the ship. I grabbed a life jacket from behind the door and struck out towards the stern where I could already see the outline of the crew, illuminated off and on by the lightning. The waves were swamping the boat to such an extent that most of the crew were engaged in a desperate struggle to free the lifeboats, the rest were punch-drunk, hanging on for sweet life. The Jaan Anvelt[16] was on her beam ends now and with no power, would be done for in minutes. When I made the stern, I looked around and saw the Captain, struggling with the davits and moved across to help.

The screaming reach of the wind made even shouted speech impossible and all the Captains directions were pointed or signalled. His eyes stared through and beyond me, like the number one he seemed to be suddenly overcome by a great weight as though newly plated with iron. We freed the last ropes from the broken davit and the Captain gestured everyone into their boats. I hopped in with Demos The Greek, the boy Sylvan and two of the engineers. We were the next to go after the large pinnace, which held at least twenty men. The Captain, the number one and the rest of the engine room let go all the boats before making ready their own and, I found out later, not one of them was seen alive again.

As for my own boat, we were immediately and comprehensively swamped by only the wash from a truly colossal wave, probably the same one that went right on to settle the Anvelt's business. In those first few moments we were all looking out for ourselves in the general panic and before we knew where we were at, young Sylvan had gone by the board. Zobrowski and the carpenter's mate (whose name I have lost) immediately dived in to save him and another wave swallowed them both. Now only Old Demos and I remained and as I desperately struggled to get my oars into the swell, the old man tried to steer in the direction of Sylvan and the others. We saw Sylvan best a wave some moments later. The other two drowned. I shipped the oars while we were dragging Sylvan out but we were hit at just the wrong moment and all but capsized, anyway we lost both the oars. Our situation was grave. The old man, Old Demos gave up steering and, with Sylvan unconscious, we spent the whole time either bailing or just steadying the boat. That we survived at all is a plain miracle. We saw no sight of any of the others who were all, it turned out, less fortunate than ourselves, even those in the pinnace. Our luck was so extreme perhaps we had cornered the market to the exclusion of everyone else, that awful night. The storm must have died away at first light and when we woke from a dead-man's sleep, the whole sea was so tea tray flat as to convince us that last night was just a cruel dream. We checked the emergency stores (the same ones I had been ordered to stow in every boat before the storm). There was enough water in carefully sealed jars for several days, some tins of food and a sopping bag of wet biscuit. There was also a small flask of spirits, which the three of us shared and emptied there and then, as though to toast our fragile thread of luck. With no stars the old Greek could not figure where exactly we might be travelling and with no oars we would have to be content simply to drift with whichever tide would have us. We were all three in a crooked state, especially the old man though he would never own to it. We shared a tin of meat and a mouthful each of the salty, sodden biscuits. Sylvan was immediately sick into the empty meat tin.

From then on, the wind kept off us mostly, apart from a short and near fatal squall on the second afternoon. The sky was cloud filled the whole time, even through the darkness so Old Demos found there were no starry compass pointers to be had, though by the rising of the sun he reckoned our path took us South-southeast. Most of our time was spent in either bailing out the boat or in lying about the boat, utterly comatose with exhaustion. Rationing the food was a hard pill to take as we were dry-tongued constantly and as ravenous as tigers.

By the fourth day we were pretty demoralized. We seemed to have entered an area of very sluggish sea and had to endure what felt like hours without number in a brute heat, turning slowly around and around as though on a spit being roasted. It was intolerable. Our food was adequate for just a few more days (Demos and I having decided on strict rationing), our water, not much longer. When that went, well, we knew for certain that without landfall we would soon perish.

We lost track of time in the intensity of that heat bowl, only guessing at the hour by the strength of the sun. We spent our days under cover of any clothes we had as exposed flesh was soon wretchedly blistered. As the slow bend of the current took us along, our health gradually began to dwindle. We were plagued by mouth ulcers, salt sore, sunburn and a continual, raging thirst because of our rationing. I gave out the last of our stores (a shared tin of fish) on our sixth evening in the boat; we were nearly out of water by the eighth, having already reduced our rations to two cupfuls a day. There was no sight, not only of land but of anything. Not even a bird or a flying fish passed us by. I felt so utterly feeble and *fragile that I could hardly move. Long, long hours spent staring out from under my blanket: at the dipping horizon, at night at the milky way, an occasional shooting star.*

Demos was growing weaker by the hour. He hardly spoke now and only emerged from under his blanket for the water ration. I think he had given up hope. Young Sylvan was looking black-faced, sun-scorched and as dried and shrivelled up as an old man. I knew we could manage without food for a considerable time. Without water in this heat, we had no chance at all.

The next few day are a hot, unbearable mess in my mind. Each of us was suffering from some fever or delirium for some of he time but the old Greek soon began to permanently rave. At one point I had to try and restrain him, which nearly cost me the last of my reserves, he was upsetting the boat. Old salt though he was, I believe Demos had resorted to drinking the sea water. That night, after venting his madness by berating me in the foulest language and then tearfully begging for forgiveness, Old Demos the Greek suddenly died.

While Sylvan slept on, oblivious, I found the strength to roll the old man over the side before I collapsed into a dreadful faint.

The crisis had come for me and the boy. We had less than two days of consciousness if our luck held. By now I was suffering the most intense pain in all my extremities, constant migraines, my tongue was so swollen as to make swallowing a struggle and constant gnawing cravings for water that I was half crazy with it. I was so often feverish that sleep became fragmented: seconds snatched here and there, awakening in fear of death.

The next day after the old man's passing we happened upon a first real piece of luck. Towards morning, in a flat calm, the clouds finally opened and a heavy shower of rain fell, which unaffected by any sea wind, was completely free of salt water. I had noticed the lie of the clouds and had found enough energy to catch more than a pint in our empty food tins. Sylvan was by now, completely unable to move at all and despite his half share of the water, I began to wonder if he would survive another night, he looked so sickly and ill. He started to become delirious a little later in the day and despite his continued attempts to rally himself, pull himself together, I could tell he was beginning to fade away. I sat by him as he worsened, tried to quieten him as much as I could. I told him we would soon reach land and helped him to the last of the water, but it seemed his constitution was all worn out. Between his bouts of unconsciousness and fever, he was often quite lucid and I was happy to hear he imagined himself back in Odessa with his mother and sister. I hope he was a little comforted. I cannot be precise as to the time and date of his passing. I believe it was somewhere towards the dawn.

I now found I had a desperate decision to make and one that I shall always regret though I am sure it saved my life. I knew that I would die unless I could find a little nourishment. One horrible recourse lay open to me and my desperate hunger (returning now, like a new curse after so recently quenching my thirst) forced my hand. I carved off and ate a small part of the dead boy's thigh. Several other pieces, my eyes wet with tears I carved off and left on the seat, to be eaten later. I slept for the rest of that day and awoke with still a slight fever (naturally, a raging thirst) and some spells of giddiness but otherwise stable enough. I continued dozing off and on until sunset, when I quickly swallowed down the rest of my gruesome store and, overcome with bitter guilt and recrimination, helped the tiny wasted form of the dead boy into the ocean. I hoped his spirit would forgive me for the horrifying thing I was forced to do.

It was just before dawn when I awoke. The boat was drifting towards the strangest sea-mist I ever saw. Perhaps some kind of effervescent algae or plankton was reflected back in the moonlight from the surface of the waves. The colour danced and sparkled all around me. Thinking back now, surely it must have been a dream vision, some hallucination brought on by my lack of food and water and the recent terror and confusion brought over me by my cannibalism. And yet I can see it still, quite clearly in my memory. I even recall looking back over my shoulder to watch that glittering cloud career off towards the darkness. Dream or no dream, the mist had brought with it the queerest feelings of timelessness, as though I had been floating on those seas and born up in that cloud ever since the first turn of the earth, as though I would always be there, floating along through a thousand lifetimes.

That morning another burst of rain fell briefly but heavily and I was able to snatch another half pint of water before I fell into the middle of a profound and healing sleep.

The chronicle of those days following the loss of the boy are odd enough now to recall, let alone to relate. Strange beyond words. The changes within my constitution brought about, I am convinced, by my last awful meal, soon began to make themselves felt. I was overwhelmed by feelings of, at times, the utmost cheerfulness, even elation, despite my circumstances and all that had recently transpired. My body felt as strong and as healthy as it had done since leaving the *Jaan Anvelt*. The bouts of fever kept returning but somehow when I did return to my senses, it seemed to leave me feeling, if any thing, even more robust. At first I put these strange developments down to the effect of my ordeal but I soon began to realize, this could hardly be the case.

I was quite bewildered by the physical changes that began to follow, one hot on the heels of the other. At first, I thought the strange numbing feeling and swelling around my chest and upper body came from the same source as my inner confusions and yet the specifics of the change could not be put down to anything in my experience. Not even the most severe water loss and then retention could produce so intense a local swelling. My chest and nipples were aching with the same intensity as childhood growing pains. When I woke from one of the strange regenerative deliriums I was now undergoing every hour or more, I would find both the pain and the distension in my breast had increased noticeably. I couldn't begin to figure out exactly what I was undergoing and if it hadn't been for those feelings of elation I mentioned, I would've begun to seriously panic. For now the strange numbing began to work its way down, away from my swollen chest and to increase dramatically around my inner thighs and private parts. With this change came a marked increase in my periods of delirium. Not ten minutes would now pass before I was again insensible and, again, when I awoke, that sense of physical enchantment an inner contentment and renewed bodily vigour. This feeling developed to such an extent that the physical changes

I was undergoing seemed to have less and less significance. I noticed with a sanguine sense of self-appraisal that my limbs had altered their formation quite beyond recognition, were more soft to the touch, supple and fine. My breasts now seemed to have swollen to their very utmost and no longer gave me any pain, indeed, I took a strange new pride in their softness and their gentle symmetry. However, the greatest transformation I had undergone was only discovered when, after a longer than usual period of unconsciousness, in standing to urinate over the side, the urine cascaded down over my thighs and down my legs. A quick search revealed that my entire genital area had undergone a shocking revolution. Then, I noticed, at the bottom of the boat, a dried and shrivelled up little bundle, lying beneath my seat. Now I realised. My genitals, my breasts, my whole person was completely altered. I had become a woman. This was far too much for my fevered brain and I immediately fell into another long period of delirium.

It was only an hour or so from that final loss of consciousness that my boat was spotted and I was rescued by a passing ship.

At the time of my rescue, I was utterly insensible. When I finally regained my consciousness, I was being cared for by the ship's doctor and the first officer, a German: Lieutenant Münster who spoke excellent Russian. After downing several long draughts of water, the Lieutenant had me sent up a bowl of soup and a hot brandy and water, which was more welcome than I can describe. The taste of the brandy alone was enough to send my senses over the edge. I was immediately, shamefully tipsy and just as quickly fast asleep.

I did not stir until the following day when I awoke alone and utterly refreshed in my small cabin. I noticed a dressing mirror and without hesitation fell to an immediate and assiduous inspection of my new design. I was still mystified and deeply confused but again found myself surprised at my own resignation, my even placid approval as to the nature of and implications of the changes. I wondered when exactly in the future it would sink in: the loss of all I had until then, taken for granted. My manhood was the axiom on which all my notions of self resided and yet, as I gazed upon my new physique and my new *countenance in the glass I admit I was moved almost to tears by my loveliness. What beautiful lines, how soft-edged, fresh and delicate my grizzled old face now was. I stood a pace back from the mirror and removed my dressing gown. I began to properly admire the rest of my novel and captivating appearance, almost from the slight remove of an appreciative student of anatomy. My curves were certainly awesome to behold. The breasts were full and yet somehow contrived to thrust themselves forwards and upwards rather than simply hanging loosely down.*

In my life up until then, I had had little or no experience of the opposite sex. In truth I was a virgin. As my eyes travelled over my recent transformations for the first time I was overcome by the most unusual feelings. I relished my beauty and was overcome by its power. Instead of the terror, the nightmare of such a transformation, it was all I could do to control my pleasure, my fingers explored every bump and curve; I couldn't tear my gaze away from the mirror, turning this way and that to capture every angle of the incredible change. The gentle incline of my buttocks, sweeping out so from my hips! How wonderful! I could easily have stood there and admired my behind all day had it not been for Lieutenant Münster's knock on the cabin door. I replaced my gown and, returning to my bed asked him to enter.

And now! What gratification to learn for the first time that I was not just beautiful to my own eyes! Lieutenant Münster was immediately, palpably entranced by my appearance. I could tell it instantly. I knew as soon as I caught his eye. He blushed, frowned and looked away almost immediately but nevertheless I could sense he regarded me as nothing less than a very beautiful woman! This new epiphany only seemed to enhance my feelings of euphoria, of stimulation. I fairly glowed in the warmth of it! Poor Lieutenant Münster was obviously a shy man and I didn't want to embarrass him. However, I couldn't help but revel in the situation a little and asked to shake his hand to thank him for taking such good care of me. As I did so I was inwardly shocked at the manifest changes to my vocal chords which, far from offering up their usual throaty rasp now sent out delightfully soft and breathy trills of sound. Lieutenant Münster didn't appear to notice anything unusual about my voice. In his shaky Russian, he said he was delighted I was coming on so well. He also hoped that the Captain might be introduced to me before the end of the day, as he was very interested in hearing all the details of my ordeal (what ship, her cargo and bearing etc.) I told the Lieutenant that I would be happy to meet the Captain at any time but was still very shaky and profoundly confused and, as to his questions, unfortunately my memory was still very vague indeed.

The next day the Lieutenant called on me again, once more in lieu of a visit from his Captain. I told him that I still felt very weak indeed, especially when I tried to recall recent events but would naturally, speak to the Captain if he deemed it absolutely vital. Lieutenant Münster assured me most kindly that I must not compromise my health in any way. He would advise the Captain to postpone my interview until the following day and even then, only under advisement from the ship's doctor who he would send to examine me again in the morning.

My prevarications were vital. Though I still felt unnaturally stimulated and giddy with excitement, I had to admit that my memory had, for the time being, completely deserted me and as things stood, I could hardly bring to my mind my own name, let alone the circumstances of the last few weeks. I needed a little more time to calm myself and to come to some form of resolution regarding who and more importantly exactly what I was. But no matter how hard I tried to get a grip on any semblance of my old self, I was invariably overtaken by that same weightlessness, similar in essence to the fainting fits I had undergone in the boat; a waking version of that same fever. Then, I would once more be drawn, with renewed delight to the mirror in my cabin and to the contemplation of…

I searched through all the other boxes, trunks and packing cases but could find no beginning and no end to this bizarre narrative. The last pages were torn out. If Internal Affairs had gotten hold of that, what would they have made of it?

(an academic point anyway, as, according to Old Nikolai they were both dead). It looked like a woman's hand? Now that I had read it, would I need to confess to it? Had it somehow attached itself to my guilty consciousness along with everything else? As I thought about all this, I thought back to my recent painting and all I could remember of it, the story of my own history. My dreams even. I could not recall even a glimmer of the floor-work when I had been in the deepest 'trance' and yet, despite my interest in finding out, in looking back, something told me I could no longer return. Whatever painted egg it was I had laid in there must hatch and die all on its own. And yet. And yet. Maybe one last look before they painted over or washed it off. But when? Perhaps one night soon? I might turn on the light in there for a few minutes, just before dawn, no-one would notice. Or in the middle of an arrest, when everyone's ears would be sharply tuned for footfalls. The awful lottery of sound that, as I write, is once more beginning…

Must we go through it again? It is truly biblical. The soldiers of Herod. The Agony in the Garden. The tramp of a Roman sandal, the soft slap of metal against leather. Isitmeisitmeisitme? Oh, Christ I know, I know. It comes upon me worse now, now I am invisible. Because I cannot really run away. No-one can. Where would they go? Where? Eh, comrade? To a dacha at Peredelkino[17]? Wrong! A train to the Caucasus? Wrong again, numbskull! It's the huge, awful fact about Russia: the sheer, unapproachable size of it! You could walk thirty miles in a day across country, hiding in ditches, avoiding people, sleeping in forests, only travelling at night! And you could walk those thirty miles for a year, ten years! A whole lifetime of walking still won't walk you out of Mother Russia. Even her history is a matter of geography.

I should just wait for all the scenarios to play themselves out: the shuffle of feet, the doorbell's ring. The 'Midnight

Call', the punched head, the broken nose. The pistol at the back of the neck scenario. The penal servitude for life scenario. And then: there is the flip side. The Waiting. Life lived under the perpetually falling sword. Carthage is surrounded and the last arrow has flown, Death stands at the citadel gates. We know he is coming, only when? Today or next year? There is a vital spark blown upon by the wind of Death's approach, his terrible promise. A spark that flares up into a last beautiful blaze of life. Every stolen moment is a reprieve granted, imbued with Death's magic but burning up from life's last embers The longer the wait goes on, the more wondrous a thing it is that I am still here at all, still standing and the Spring I am watching, smelling, tasting is the quintessence of Springs: a distillation. The early morning mists, the soft rain, the sky as pure as an angel's tear. My heart breaks with it, it truly does. And that, I suppose, is some consolation.

Meanwhile, the dreams continue on.

Once more last night I was some weird water spirit, without even a body of my own. I became somehow embedded in the giant brain of a whale and felt myself a part of its whole system, its great soft weight, even its consciousness. I inhabited all the caverns, the vast warm spread of its body mass as it surged onwards. It is true that I have always wondered about the thoughts of whales, how much they know and feel. Like elephants, I imagined their thoughts were like them: heavyweight, ancient and ponderous, like old wise men. Now I was part of the soft tissue surrounding the whale's cortex I could know all this if I wanted to, but in fact was so busy enjoying the insuperable power of the whales glide through the ocean that I had quite forgotten to try and inhabit its thoughts. What were they? When I finally got round to it, I was surprised by the flexibility of its mind, its bright sense of excitement and the same delight in its own passage as I was feeling. Such sharp reflexes and reactions! It was more like a bucking horse than a great leviathan! I realised my hostess was still only a young calf, happy to be in motion, making waves and pushing the water around, going deeper, swimming faster, relishing this moment. Through its eyes I looked out into the deep black blue expanse and was again surprised, this time by the searing clarity of its vision, as though she could spy a single, distant krill. We rolled and turned about through the current and then careered up to pocket some more breath. I was breathing for the first time, at least that was how it felt. There was a storm here again and I relished it from protection of the whale. The giant rollers towered and hollowed out as though the whale's lungs were a great big bellows, at work under the surf. In the near distance I saw a lighthouse beam circle from the top of a cliff and, in the dream I was thrilled to see signs of human life. A second later and the whale was diving down again as far and as deep as it could into the darkest, blackest blue at the heart of the dream.

This dream I have had in many variations over the last few days. Always underwater (a relief from the storms and winds!) and always somehow subsumed within the mind of one living thing or another: a giant squid, a dolphin. But mostly I seemed to inhabit the consciousness of that same female whale. At one point, I remember the whale within whose mind I rode, being covered by a shadow, a huge looming shape that blocked out the light. I realised it was another whale, a massive bull, whose tail brushed delicately against her dorsal fin. Distracted, I thought they must be teaming up to hunt for herring, I did not realize that these were the preludes to a coupling. In all the excitement, as the male dived and capered, sending up a surge of bubbles; my grip was loosened and I felt a kind of vertigo at the thought of being loosened, cast out to become another passing element of the ocean. Now I was just a part of the whale's body. I only fully understood what was happening when the bull's seed collided with the egg. As the bull broke away and headed into deeper water with a final squeal of satiation, I felt a return to normality. The egg fertilized, my whale gently dozed and let the tide carry her.

The pregnancy only seemed to last for seconds before she was giving birth, though I could somehow recall the thrill of feeling the foetus grow within us. I found I could inhabit not just its developing body but also the wide-openness, the deep lacuna of its mind and enjoyed the great solace and quiet of a sea within a sea. When the baby came at last, I was still asleep and born inside it.

Only three weeks ago, I was walking back from my job at the Artists Union for some time off (as recommended by the *bastard* Tumanov. He whose eyes betrayed him. Informer! Bumlicker!). I shuffled through the snow, gave my hellos to Old Nikolai and plodded up the stairs. As I was coming around the corner into the corridor, there was an old woman I had never seen before at the far end trying to coax a small black and white cat over to be stroked. The cat had just allowed the old lady's hand to run along its prickle of fur and right at that moment it caught sight of me. For some reason I decreased my pace and stayed my footfall for fear of somehow ruining the moment, either for the old lady or the cat, or both together. It was then that I knew I would never leave the flat again. Not until they came to take me. Something in the gentleness of that meeting of fur and skin sent me scuttling into my den forever. Typical. I, who have been surrounded by enemies, who have faced cavalry charge and massed artillery, no end of imperialist bullets, finally brought to bay by the sight of an old lady and a kitten.

I still haven't painted a thing in here yet and I still feel as though I never shall. No energy left, the sap has dried, is drained. Maybe one really can become painted out. The question arises: what need to keep painting if enough has been said? Yet I cannot see what it is I have done (I mean next door, those last days of unconscious daubing. Perhaps all I have left is an aberration? A shit smear. Yet I had that feeling in the pit of my stomach during its making that something was glowing, an effervescence in the air. Perhaps that's all it was, a sparkle in the dust, a foamy blur and then, nothing worthwhile to remain. Either way I have resolved that I must break back in, if only to see what it was I had actually *said* with the paint. I will bide my time, by God! Wait for the right moment. When there is enough distraction, enough banging of doors.

As I said, I found no more writing in the boxes but this was not the only thing of interest. Hundreds and hundreds of tiny sepia photographs, what must have been the previous tenants families, whole histories. I have now discovered their names: they were the Karpins: Grigori Nikolayevich and Nadya Iosifovna Karpin. Not unusually, for me, I had never managed to catch a glimpse of them in the few weeks they had been there, so I could only attempt to guess at who they might be. Lying there under the sepia was a dark faced and rather shifty eyed man, tall and backwardsfallingly elegant in white suit and tennis shoes. He seemed a good candidate and reoccurred a lot, as did a snub-nosed young woman with page boy hair and a blazing, toothy smile. Was this them? And was it this young woman who had dared the loony story of the man changing into a woman? I found it hard to fathom. And yet it had significance. Something like that, out of the blue is always sending a message. I think so anyway. A book found on a train, a letter picked up off the street. They arrive for a reason and should not be taken lightly. I re-read the whole story last night. Is it an allegory? A red herring or a shaggy dog?

I forgot to say, I did find one other book when I was very delicately freeing up the big room to paint on and moving the telephone, the book fitted so precisely under its base that I suspected it might be anti-soviet propaganda, a treatise by Trotsky or Bukharin. It turned out to be harmless: the Russian translation of a Yankee novel by one Mark Twain called *The Adventures of Tom Sawyer*. It was the picaresque story of a naughty American hoodlum, filled with various daring japes, jaunts and capers. But what really had me at sixes and sevens (admittedly at this point it hardly took much) was a passage I read there about a painting: the painting of a large fence with whitewash. Somehow the story had me coming over decidedly odd. Perhaps I was reading too much into what I perceived was meant to be a story for children but there was something of Death, of Nothingness in that great wooden wall of white. And yet the mischievous soul of a child poked Death's nose for it and tricked one after the other of his friends into the task, a task which seemed to foreshadow every grown-up task, every burdensome, workaday reality in their lives to come. Those saps, his friends were welcome to it! He knew better.

The story struck me and brought back to me the memory of a certain incident I was involved in during the worst winter of the war.

The Division, *my* Division was lined up for an attack on a large detachment of White troops defending a nameless town somewhere on the Dnieper (which was frozen over). They were well dug in and with a usefull amount of artillery. Still, they were a raggletaggle bunch. Not that we could boast, what with winter having sunk her teeth into the year, the glorious Army of the Revolution was up to its cruppers in shit, frostbite and frozen horses. A large part of our regiment was made up of Anarchists from the so-called Black Army[18] who most of us would only trust as far as we could throw them (imagine, not believing in anything?) On paper the attack was meant to take place under a creeping barrage of our artillery although, of course, we were all only too well aware that most of our big guns had been carted off to a more important part of the front, to deal with a massive White Army counterattack.

As I lifted my frozen snout over the parapet all I could see was steppe, disappearing into a truly perfect white: snow meeting a wall of ice-mist. A terrifyingly blank canvas on to which a rather grizzly scene was about to be painted, the images from which had passed before my eyes too many times already: the steam rising from the entrails of a pony, the pat of bullets hitting already dead bodies, the last curse and the last rattle. I had made winter attacks before, sometimes even at night and the terror is indescribable. I always hoped everyone else felt the same and that it wasn't just me. The only way to know for sure exactly where you were going was to head right into the bullets. Nights like that, with the wind at your back, the snow flying and the ground shifting and bouncing with the explosions, gravity begins to play funny tricks and you start to feel as though you are not walking upright at all anymore but falling, down, down into the Devil's maw, and he is worrying at you like a tattered rag. But, be all that as it may, that morning, my Officer was Konstantin Konstantinovich of famous memory! He Who Laughed At Everything And Feared Nothing.

I knew from taking down the orders the previous night that the Brigadier had 'requested' our Konstantin to organise a small feint attack on the far left flank, utilizing the anarchist's *tachankas*[19] and one or two small artillery pieces they had already lifted from the Whites. The main thrust was going to be at the centre right of the village. In these conditions it would be impossible for the enemy to know exactly how many were attacking; a squad of men on horseback going full tilt and screaming like bearded harpies would feel like a whole battalion. Konstantin Konstantinovich was to get up as close as he could with the cannon and two heavy machine guns and pester their flank for half an hour, before the main dash right at them.

Now this Konstantinovich was what you would call an 'individual' he was as staunch a soldier as you could wish, tight as a drum in a pinch and all of us loved him, from his frozen nose to the tip of his spurs. There was something cavalier and do-as-you-like about the tilt of his fur cap and the way he wore his *shaska*[20] everywhere he went (he being of Cossack blood). For a slap on the back from him, the men would lay down their lives with a grin. Anyway, as soon as Konstantin Konstantinovich had heard out the General with that rather cynical smile he carried, and offered a salute he headed round for a confidential chat with Oleg The Pony, not a horse but a man, or to be exact a *mouth*. Oleg The Pony had the biggest gob this side of the Urals and Konstantin went to ask him for a piece of advice. He came straight out and told him that he had been asked to put together a top secret mission across enemy lines and he needed only the maddest, most foolhardy and brave hearted men in the squad. I wanted to ask you first, comrade, said Konstantinovich to Oleg The Pony, because you always know what's what. Well! Out with it! Who do you recommend? They talked the whole thing over and in parting, old Konstantin told him to be a good fellow and keep it under his hat.

Of course, when he came out of his quarters, by the stable, the following morning, there were fifty men with horses lined up under the trees! Even Old Oleg himself, the vagabond, and that was how I found out what had happened in the attack, from The Pony himself, while he was waiting to die, layed out on the remains of an old cart, smoking his pipe. Almost all the others had got it in the neck during the attack, which they kept up for two hours. Our main attack had been beaten back but the fire had been so constant from Konstantin and his men that the Whites had been forced to overplay their hand and had counterattacked. This opened up a gap half a *verst* wide. That mad bastard Konstantin Konstantinovich! said Oleg. Right up until he stopped one he was gigging like a schoolgirl! You know what his laugh was like! Infectious! Pretty soon we were all at it! It put the fear of God into the enemy, every time there was a lull in the fighting, all they could hear was our laughter!

They would've given Konstantinovich the Posthumous Medal for Valour only just a week earlier he had tried to steal the General's horse after a drunken bet and had nearly ended up against a wall. His wife was a great actress in Petrograd, and (Oleg said) as pretty as a prayer.

I wonder would he have made it up to now, like me? All I remember through all those years of war is terror, terror. It took away all my doubts, my self-regard. By that time I was well acquainted with Fear. Not Konstantin. Certainly he was never one to keep his opinions to himself. I am sure that if he had survived, he would certainly prefer a bullet than have to hide in a neighbours apartment, too angry to leave, too scared to stay. He was a proper lion. I am just a mouse in a hole.

Konstantin loved the Party more than his own life, as he proved. He always hated the idea of its leaders, even Lenin. The idea of the Great Leader, of *personality* appalled him. The individual is dead, comrade! He would laugh like a young girl when I threw up my hands in dismay at the latest set of battle orders. But his hatred of the Tsarists gave him wings! We can't go wrong, he would say, not if we are always on top of them, kicking their White arses back across the border, like Ivan the Terrible with the mongrel horde!

Anyway he's dead now along with his story. I met his wife

not long after, by the way, at the Meyerhold. She was an admirable person and indeed, beautiful. She was as quiet as the tomb until she hit the stage at which point she would explode like a howitzer round! May God keep her safe. I never mentioned having fought alongside her dead husband. What good would it do to be reminded? Not long after that little skirmish on the Dnieper, I was bayoneted through the thigh at Barguzin. What with that and the bout of typhus that followed on its tail, I was sent to recoup, up the line. This was around the time of the Great Siberian Ice March[21] after even Kolchak himself had been shot down like a dog and thrown in the river. As I headed back up the line to the field hospital, huddled in the sleigh under a foot of fur and blankets I saw the lines of frozen bodies down at the edge of Lake Baikal. Men, women and children. It was there that I lost my nerve with Russia. I knew the extermination of the opposition was setting some kind of precedent and I pitied anyone else who stood in the way of the Revolution. The policy had worked and would be a difficult option to bypass in the future. A few years later it was the *kulaks* and after that natural enough that it should be our turn. The vanguard becomes the Old Guard and the train rolls forward along the frozen bones. From then on, all I wanted to do was paint. Painters are harmless. In Russia they are overlooked - this is the age of sculptors in stone. It is rumoured that even The Great Stalin fears a poet's flourish worse than the hand of death. More than anything, when I think back to those long grey columns of the dead, I believe that the Russian earth itself had overcome them, that the country was feeding off its own.

Outside, a hot wind is blowing from the West and the apartment feels oppressive. I have to open a window, even though I might be observed at any moment. Strangely, my courage appears to be growing albeit by the tiniest accretions, like the first wet bumps of a stalagmite in a limestone cave. I even kept the light on last night to write some of this. Could it be that I no longer fear the approach of death? Not fully. And yet I am more resolved that so it must be. I think that, writing here about Konstantin's death, about the Ice March, has properly focused my mind. In the morning I will definitely try to continue my painting in this surrogate space.

I fell asleep and the dream was waiting. The sea, as thick and grey as cold larva, was surprisingly gentle even in the tooth of the wind. As I watched from high up on the cliff overlooking the bay, great flotillas of debris passed and re-passed: what looked like a whole tree, the back half of a cart with the dead packhorse still harnessed, all miraculously still afloat. The warm wind that whipped around the corner of the cape had a rasping edge, it squeezed the breath from my mouth and I felt the first, vague stirrings of my asthma. Cuppying down behind a boulder not only was I free of the wind but I also found a clear view across the bay from the gap in the rocks. A herring gull stood out in the breeze for a few moments, held me in its lizard's eye, then banked sharply, wheeling away as the sun flared out through the rain. I turned, looking out to sea and saw a rainbow rear up and then vanish.

From round the nearest reaches of the tide came what at first I couldn't distinguish, some kind of tall wooden structure. It was born up by what looked like a gimcrack timber raft, splintered at the edges. The whole thing wobbled in the swell. A window flopped open and banged against the clapboard panels. It was part of a house. I watched it brave the edge of the rollers, rocking now to such an extent that it looked set to topple over, then only just settling back; that window banging silently in the roar of the wind, at each dip and lunge. Eventually it made its precarious way to the shallows just out of his view at the bottom of the cliff. I got up to go and was immediately buffeted by the passage of the wind careering over the top of the boulder. Again, it took the breath from right out of my lungs and again I panicked briefly. I ducked down as I walked to avoid the worst.

The descent to the sand didn't offer any view at all, covered as I was on both sides with rocks and gorse. I slipped a couple of times in my rush to get there. It was still a good five minutes before I was down at the sand and even then there were more rocks to climb over and a small promontory to round before I could discover if the strange apparition had bested the tide. There it was. It stood perfectly upright, having come to rest right at the lip of the sea, still rocking slightly as the last reaches of the tide ran under its shattered base. I looked up and down the empty beach, all that was there was the rain, coming down fiercely now, vertically.

I stepped into the shallows, sopping my boots with cold sea, then gingerly, up onto the platform. The lower windows were all broken up and the left hand side, as I peered round, was a mess of smashed up spars, cracked plaster and great black gaps in the frame. A number seven was painted in free hand by the side of the door. The whole structure shook dangerously in the wind. I slipped about on the slimy deck as I edged towards the door. It pushed open a little way, enough to take a glance inside. The only light came from a low hole right at the back, over which the waves steadily lapped. Sniffing the sea and wet wood, I pushed a little harder, a disembowelled settee was blocking the door. I pushed again using my shoulder and the gap gradually widened enough to slide some light through, revealing a table, a broken chair and a mess of smashed crockery, rocking about in three inches of surf. Edging in around the dead sofa I noticed some stairs, damaged but intact and I tacked towards them, across the wet boards, only just grabbing on to the rail as the whole thing teetered again in the swell. On the first floor the clanging shutter let in erratic bursts of the day on to a ruckled old map of the Southern Ukraine and a cheap rug lying in a sodden halo of red dye. The door to the top floor was blocked as well, this time by a heap of rubbish and wet newspapers and again I forced the sopping mass back with the door. Half the steps up were missing and I could see black waves down through the splintered gape of the hole. With both hands grasping the handrail and keeping close to the wall I heaved himself upwards over the chasm. The stairs opened straight out onto the top floor, which appeared fairly dry. There were no windows but by what light there was, I could make out a small day bed in the opposite corner and the twinkling eyes of a small boy, who seemed to have just woken up.

Morning. I am quite unable to enter the old flat. Someone else (I can hear them) is sitting in there. An hour ago they even put on one of my gramophone records (Schubert! A piece from the *Schwanengesang*![22]) What are they doing? I have been unable to move for several hours. The walls are so very thin and that parquet doesn't help. They would've heard the drop of a match. I am writing this very slowly, with a soft pencil.

What are they up to?

Whoever it is has just been sitting there (after all there is only one chair) Doing what? Looking at the paintings? There is an occasional smoker's cough. Who else would have the key but the new concierge?

DIARY OF THE NEW CONCIERGE

On Friday the news came through. Levin rang to tell me. Apparently the last incumbent had been a bad sort. One of the old cadres, according to Levin. On behalf of Uncle (and his contacts), Levin offered me the job there and then. And now here I am, a concierge. My situation? Certainly my room is bare enough and the ghost of my predecessor haunts it still. Shag tobacco and some other fousty old man's smell that I can't define: not quite mothballs, more of a faded masculine smell, like a dessicated civet. Anyway it weighs upon the space. I need to burn some sugar to defeat the smell but cannot find any in the kitchen. I washed the floors, painted the walls and dusted everywhere but still that old man lingers. Perhaps it's me? Must remember to hide this diary. Been here two nights and the place has certainly been busy. I was woken by the noise both Friday and Saturday. Then the bell went. NKVD both times. Both times the same man asking where so and so's apartment was. First time, I said in all honesty that I did not know, being new to the job but if he would care to examine the large board behind him with everyone's name and apartment number on it he might find who he was looking for there. He didn't even turn round to look. Lit a cigarette and made one of his men check. I think he thought I was being a smart arse. Come Saturday night, I was ready for him. He asked for a certain name and wanted to know the flat and I (who had spent a good part of the morning noting down every single name in every single apartment, man, woman, children, pets, occupation etc. etc. on three sides of foolscap), I was ready. I do not want to find myself in trouble. Not that Uncle couldn't handle it for me, he being so close to we-all-know-who. But cousin Levin tells me things change quickly over there, despite what Uncle is always saying. Can it really be so bad?

Well it certainly is a good feeling to know I have these pages to confide in. At the last place, I had that terrible moment when I thought I had lost my previous diary. Not that it was *incriminating* or anything, just my secret thoughts. Nothing much to report today. Met a few of the tenants. I notice they dare not ask me what happened to the last concierge, Nikolai, though I knew they were all dying to. Not that I could throw any light on the matter. Hard labour, probably. Rehabilitation in a penal colony. Siberia. They all of them have a frightened look, as if they all have something to hide. Do I have that look?

The police came again last night and left with a couple: a man and a woman. I was sat at reception, reading, so I saw the agents come in and then go out. The NKVD all looked the same age as me or younger. In their early twenties mostly. The couple I had never seen before were much older. Middle age. They looked like death. He crying, she as white as ice.It was as though these ruddy-faced boys were playing at arresting their own grandparents.

Uncle came over last night, a surprise visit. He seemed chirpy enough at first but grew less convivial as he got drunker, all the time scratching off the wet label with his nail. I tried to change the subject but he didn't seem to notice, just kept on and on about 'The Situation'. It seems Levin was right; Uncle's boss is in some kind of filthy mess. Uncle, as he always does when he's drunk, began to peddle out one lame aphorism after another. 'When the axe falls, chips fly' etc. I tried to make light of it; I said I didn't know why he was complaining, he has such a cushy job over there and the boss has Stalin's ear. I said I didn't believe they would start turning on each other. What would that accomplish? But Uncle grew fractious. He told me I was a fool and knew nothing, was a whippersnapper etc. People turn on each other all the time, he slurred, if they are looking weak, suspect, you have to join in and stamp them down with the rest! Rotten trees need to be felled etc. Any slowcoaches when it comes to backstabbing are suspected of sympathising and the whole process starts up again! He stumbled off eventually after finishing the bottle. Left me with a slur of parting advice that I should keep my wits about me in this new job, I was the eyes and ears of the authorities. If you smell a rat, point him out to me, he said. I said of course Uncle and helped him to the door of his car where his driver took over. He seemed used to it. Uncle took one bleary-eyed look at this man and suddenly started raining curses down, trying to give him his boot, to punch his head. The driver was completely undaunted and stood there in the melting snow until Uncle had exhausted himself. I found it hard to watch such behaviour. Uncle was acting like an animal, like some feudal prince with a serf. I was going to remonstrate with him but, as I say this driver, Ivanoff seemed utterly indifferent, as though he was made of stone. An ex-ironworker, a blacksmith; I wonder what he thought of it? His parents probably *were* serfs! He was sure to have fought against the Tsar. Now his job involved being regularly beaten by one of the people's representatives. I wanted to sit down and break bread, drink a glass of tea with him but as he shut the door on the now comatose Uncle, he didn't even glance up at me. Probably thought I was uncle's toady nephew, which in a sense, I am. I mean I would never have got this job without Uncle's say-so. He being the head of something or other at Internal Affairs, working directly under the famous Yezhov. Even drinks with him, though that's not saying much, Uncle drinks with everyone! He calls him, this Yezhov 'The Black Dwarf' though I saw them once on a podium together for some rally for the Youth Communist League and they seemed to be getting on famously enough from where I was standing. Perhaps Uncle is treated by his boss the way he treats Ivanoff? Then, when Ivanoff himself returns home, he does the same to his wife, who beats the kid, who kicks the dog, 'Fido you numbskull! What do you mean by being a dog and living in a kennel? Who gave you permission to chew on that bone you imbecile?' Back in my room, I felt oppressed by the memory of Uncle the whole evening. That was the last time I sensed the presence of Old Nikolai though! I cannot blame his ghost for leaving, Uncle can be terrifying enough just for mere mortals.

So many nocturnal visits, I have lost count. Doesn't even wake me anymore. I had begun to get on reasonable terms with a man from the third floor. He even shared his flask of soup on the way home from work last week. The awful thing was, well, I caught his eye last night as he was being led away and that really levelled me. The prisons must be full to bursting! Nobody comes back once they have been taken away. I plucked up the courage to ask Uncle about it and he studiously ignored me. Only topping up his usual parting advice with 'and don't ask so many imbecile questions!' The last glance of that man has stayed with me. He had even managed an embarrassed smile. My God, I felt awful.

Bloody nosebleeds! Ever since I came here I have been pestered with them. As to the whys and wherefores of this misfortune, what is causing them, I am completely in the dark. Could it be a nervous reaction? All these dreadful nights? My diet has been excellent since I began and there is plenty of salad stuff just coming up from the garden. The old man Nikolai had a little vegetable patch which I intend to re-plant. I have been eating fresh bread, fruit and even the odd piece of chicken.

Yesterday I woke to find my pillow damp and cold with my own blood, what looked like pints of the stuff! It was really shocking. I must try and see a Doctor; there is a small hospital on the seventh floor. Aside from that, the building committee held a meeting today and have decided on a new fire alarm, as the old system is a joke: a big bell on each landing! The kids are ringing them all the time and people no longer notice the sound. In the meeting I was told I must draft a letter to each resident, informing them of the date and time of the first test. New laws require every citizen to assemble outside the building at a muster station and to leave each flat open to inspection. It is not as much work as it sounds. There are usually about five hundred flats but, at the moment, only half of these are actually occupied.

Anyway at the very least it will break the monotony and allow me to properly meet some of the residents.

Another n.b! I had nodded off in the reception office, listening to music on the old wireless. When I woke up my vest was soaked in blood. Where is it all coming from?

Fairly boring days (only the nights are horrible). Today's major incident? The post woman was complaining because she couldn't fit any more letters into the mail box belonging to a certain V. Buryatin. I took several weeks of mail from the box and put it in the drawer of my bureau for safekeeping.

Having spent most of yesterday drafting the letters to every resident, I went up and delivered them all by hand. Tried to make sure my knock was as unofficial as possible (with a friendly rat-ta-tat-TAT!) But still, those faces! Like old, cold porridge! Occasionally a child would answer, a welcome relief from all the wary grey mugs owned by everyone over ten years old. Most received the letter and my greetings with no more than a wary nod of comprehension. I knocked at V. Buryatin's but no answer and left the letter under the door. I could have sworn I heard someone in there!

My cousin Levin came over last night for a chat and some drinks. He bought some cold chicken and a bottle of vodka, which we made a heavy dent in. I told him about Uncle and how shocked I was at the way he had behaved towards his own driver. Levin was not surprised, only saddened. He said that my Uncle (his Father) was trying to drink himself to death because he lacked the courage to put the gun in his mouth. He said my Aunt 'Talia had been forced to stay with relatives in the South it had gotten so bad. He said that the regime at Internal Affairs was in a state of complete flux. Stalin had lost faith in the People's Commissar General Yezhov and the rest of the Central Committee were out for his hide, wanted 'his balls on a stick' as Levin put it. He said what you don't understand Sanya is how vulnerable he is, how vulnerable we all are. I mean, think about it, he said, that's the way it seems to work, no? If you are seen to have gone rotten then you might easily have infected others. All one's associations are implicated. Cauterise! Cauterise! Father is being slowly driven mad by it, he said and that driver, that Ivanoff has to carry a pistol at all times just in case Father is arrested. They have a drill so Father can do what needs to be done before his old cadres get him in for questioning. Once, said Levin, when he was drunk he started to talk about what goes on over there. Torture, executions by the score. It is killing him Sanya. I am sure he can't even think back to a time before all this; we both know he was a different man. This was certainly true. Poor Uncle! I remember when he used to

take me and Levin fishing in the lake by their *dacha*. Taught us how to bait the hook, how to cook a catfish. He would take the hook from the fish's wet mouth *so* very gently.
A different man. He's a different man alright. I tried to change the subject. I asked how things were with Levin at the Air Ministry, which was, of course a stupid gambit, he starts going on about the threat of war, how we are unprepared, how everyone is too young and inexperienced, how there are not enough Generals, what the projected casualties were etc. We soon became silent enough after that and ate some of the chicken, with some salt and that good bread.

It was only when I started asking him about his fiancée and their plans for the marriage that I finally got a smile out of him. He is in love, the poor fool and good luck to him! At least it tempers some of those worries about the future, after all its not all doom and gloom!

Been too busy all week to get half a chance to sit down and write my thoughts and now that I come to sit down and write them, I find there is nothing there to be said. Too busy even for that. Nothing much of import though until the day of the tests, today, which has been an amazing one and I will tell all about that in a minute. The week was unusually quiet, even at night there were no arrests for a change. Lots of work for me tying up loose ends, all the flats that have been unoccupied (often still filled with belongings) were signed off last Wednesday. I was given a comprehensive list of apartments to clean out, to either store or dispose of the belongings. I had to break open the seal on each door left by the police which said something about the contents of this flat were art of an investigation and it was illegal to tamper etc. There were twenty-eight of these flats to be cleaned out, pending the arrival of new owners I suppose.

I only got round to doing five, which is still pretty good going. The rest I will do when I can. They were very specific about the flats being left completely spotless. Whitewashed walls, clean floors & windows. No curtains, no linen, nothing but bare floors, bath and stove. I must admit that I felt too guilty to keep much of anything from the empty flats. It felt like bad luck. Only what tinned and dried food I could find, coffee, soap, a few books (anyway none of them were great readers). All a bit depressing. Anyway, at least the tests went off without any real hitch.

The bell went off right on the nose of midday, an official took the roll call while Superintendent Dubkhov and I went through all the rooms. On the 9th floor, at the apartment of that same V. Buryatin the door was still locked (which Superintendent Dubkhov was utterly furious about!). I had the master keys for every room. What a sight when we opened the door!

Is this Buryatin a madman or a genius? Either way he has disappeared and no notice from Internal Affairs as to his status. He hasn't been seen for several weeks past. But what splendour! What a wonderful jungle of colour! We had only a few moments to look about us and both of us were speechless, even that miserable old tight arse, Dubkhov. The bedroom was filled with nearly all the furniture, the rolled up carpets (he had even painted the floor!) And bizarrely, in the bedroom, what looked like a mural by another artist. But the detail! I would have to come back and look again when things are quieter. We could only linger a moment.

As we left, Superintendent Dubkhov was already talking about whitewashing over the walls. I could not believe he was in earnest. I had to keep mum. The rest of the day was pretty uneventful. I cleared out another apartment on the seventh floor.

Superintendent Dubkhov arranged to call on me earlier today and we went back up to the Buryatin apartment, to plan our next move, as he put it. He was understandably nervous about the situation. I should tell you about my superior, this Dubkhov. The House Superintendent and Chairman of the House Committee is not perhaps the finest specimen of Soviet manhood. He is the sort of low-level official who, in the usual run of things is unremittingly rotten to any underling. That should have meant me but he knew my Uncle and I suspect Uncle had warned him to treat me with kid gloves. Therefore with me he is always obsequious, unctuous to the extreme, a little too much oil with the salad! Everything was: would you do me the great favour of…this, or: do me the honour of allowing me to request… that. But behind those shrew's eyes, I sense the blackest hatred. I will have to stay on his good side. Anyway, Dubkhov said that rather than stir up any trouble with Internal Affairs, (who he seemed to know a lot about?) we should wait a short time to see what might happen. The most likely event would be that in a few days we would get the nod from the proper authorities regarding his whereabouts. It was impossible for us to act until then because this Buryatin might, at any moment pop up like the proverbial jack-in-the box. Dubkhov said we should leave the whole thing alone for at least a week or so and then discreetly inform the authorities that Buryatin had disappeared, seemingly without leaving a trace. The flat certainly didn't look as though anyone would be wanting to move back in to it; that is not to say it was dirty, apart from two large sacks of rubbish which I had to take out to the refuse chute. If anything, it was much cleaner than most. So, as far as Dubkhov's concerns were concerned, everything suited me fine (though I found it very hard to concentrate on what he was saying in that wholly unreal environment; I longed for some time alone with these images to try and understand the story). The upshot was that we wait at least a short while before the full whitewash. Superintendent Dubkhov having finished for the day and tottered off to his own place upstairs, I have just been back up to the Buryatin apartment for an hour or so. I found a wind-up gramophone and listened to some German music (there are empty flats both sides so no concern about noise).

I need to describe it all, as I saw it, while it's fresh in my mind.

Now, as one enters the flat one is immediately in an L-shaped corridor, at the bottom part of the L. The bedroom with the Revolutionary mural is on the right. On the left is a high window then, in two rooms along the left of the 'L': first the kitchen and then further along, the bathroom. At the right, opposite the bathroom at the end of the long corridor, is the door to the front room. In my mind I already remember it as 'The Sistine Chapel'. There is a high window on the left hand side as one enters and the wall to one's right is the biggest, the main wall. Absolutely every single spare inch of ceiling, floor and wall space has been decorated in paint: but the most finely detailed paintings you could imagine, which seem to start some rough chronology in the hall as one enters. The kitchen has also been filled with images. The only spaces left bare are a little bit of the bathroom, which is partially tiled. All the carpets, chairs, a sofa, shelves and cupboards have been removed and left in a big pile in the bedroom. The only furniture is a table on wheels that has been used as a palette, a large stepladder and an old leather armchair in the centre of the living room. The whole thing was painted in the most delicate washes of colour. It smelt like oil paint but seemed to have been applied like watercolour and with the tiniest brushes. The whole effect is difficult to describe. At times, I remember it felt subterranean but thinking about it now, my memory is similar to the memory of being underwater, having dived to the bottom of some deep pool. As one got in amongst the detail, it appeared to represent an attempt at a life history, presumably of the owner, this V. Buryatin.

What was it I saw? Thinking back, it felt like a brief glimpse of the very fabric of memory itself but perhaps I am exaggerating? There were a thousand painted incidents and occurrences that seemed straightforward enough, others I could not possibly comprehend. Every few yards this supposedly sequential order of events would loop off into what appeared to be the landscape of a dream. Then the two strands would seem to commingle and then zip away again into separate strands and identities, each with a non-linear momentum of its own, only to again collide further along the wall. By the time the painting arrived in the kitchen I felt I was being born aloft on the wave of its cascading harmonies and its incredibly subtle colouration. The tone dipped down suddenly darker with burnt umbers and frosty greys when the painting entered a dream/memory of the war. I thought I could discern Lake Baikal and there was the execution of the Tsar and his family at Yekaterinburg (could this Buryatin have been actually *present?*). The painting seemed to burst into flower again at the Tenth Party Congress[23]. There was something epic, something truly Russian about the scale, as though there was a gigantic endlessness in the depth of the detail. It made the inside of my head feel…vast! As though not just me but every Russian citizen is their own, personal steppe! The intermingling of memory of history and of dream seemed to open up great, long vistas of thought and feeling and when I turned right at the end of the corridor and beheld the epic splendour of that last great room, it took my breath away. Perhaps it was the effect of the spring light that was flooding the room but it felt that the painting had truly reached its apogee against that big end wall, as though it had finally taken wings and flown.

After a long look at the wall and the ceiling, my eyes fell naturally to the floor and especially towards the corner. Something really extraordinary had happened here and it took me a long time to pinpoint what it was that was going on. I don't mean just at that moment. I came back many times to examine that corner and what really piqued my interest; apart from the extraordinary quality of the painting was that in several places, running through the painted narrative, I could discern *my own face and figure*!

You see it came upon me there quite suddenly, that somewhere in the middle of the parquet, the painting had come completely up to date. Here was a painting of a man *painting*, amongst all the floating dimensions of dream and memory and at that point the language of the paint became fractured, more gestural. Nonetheless, a pattern, a story within the mass could still be discerned. Yes, it was I, in my new boiler suit and mess of hair, looking at those same paintings. Then a rising sense of panic as I saw that, at a point not inches from where I stood, Buryatin had ceased to paint history and begun painting, not just the present but also, eerily, his own notion of a possible future. It began to feel like opening buried treasure and now, if my mind's eye followed the outlines and tiny flotillas of narrative correctly, it appeared that Buryatin the painter had (inadvertently?) betrayed himself. According to his own map of imagery, he was at that moment, hiding behind a sofa in the empty apartment next door! And what was this?

I had to stop. My nose began to gush blood all over the painting and I was forced to sit down in the only chair and mingle several pints of my own blood with a half empty bucket of turpentine. I felt as weak as a newborn foal and not just with the blood loss. I had seen an image of myself with bloody nose at the exact moment the first drip hit the floor! The sudden untrammelled access into another man's thoughts and my own unknown actions had left me reeling. Could I be mistaken? Were these scenes just a part of a dream sequence? No! I looked back at that part of the painting and, there I was, just as I was. I felt sure in my bones that this Buryatin lay just behind the wall. I had to speak to him about these miraculous images, these uncanny, painted prophecies! I shuffled to the door and downstairs for the master key. I can recall running into Superintendent Dubkhov on the ground floor, outside my door. I wondered why he looked so horrified until I remembered the nosebleed: my face and chin were saturated in blood, my nose still gushing. Dubkhov waited outside while I cleaned myself with a warm flannel and found a fresh handkerchief to try and stem the flow. He had brought a new list of names, flats to be cleaned out, some going back several months. I know about the list because I found it later on the bureau, with dry drips and a bloody thumbprint. I must have fallen unconscious only one or two moments after he left. Apparently, two of the cleaners found me.

Anyway, when I woke up there was Levin with his sad, kind eyes, sat in the bedside chair, reading the paper. He explained that I was only a couple of floors up, in the little hospital-cum-surgery and had been unconscious long enough for him to be called. There is no escape for you,

Sanya! laughed Levin. Even the white sheets of a hospital lie within this fortress of ice! The blood, he told me, had refused to stop flowing until about an hour and a half ago and apparently the Doctor had given me something new called a transfusion, which meant, Levin explained, that they had had to top-up my low supplies of blood with the blood of someone else's. In this case: his! (I noticed the bandage on his rolled up sleeve). I wondered who would top-up all of *his* blood but was too weak to enquire. Levin said that I was to rest for a few days, at least until they were sure of no infections from the transfer. I was very tired and, after I had been looked over by the Doctor, I fell asleep.

The moon is full and looming up over my shoulder from across the room, from over the town. One young tubercular, still awake like me, is hacking out a cough with every few soft shakes of the gaming dice he rolls out onto his lap. Levin was right. There is no escaping this place. It feels as though one could live one's whole life without leaving this marble island, never again to taste the air. After all, everything, the whole world is here! A lifetime of supplies in the food store; a cinema, a kindergarten. Fittingly, there is even a one-room morgue. But it feels oppressive, haunted. It is, after all, a cannibal island, busy eating its own.

How excruciating! Here I am now, trying to write this by moonlight and wondering about the painter, Buryatin. Wondering what would happen to him if I opened the door on his secret. Perhaps I should leave him alone. But then, if they find him (which of course they will) won't he be arrested? I'm not sure what for… trespassing? What about his painting and his hermitude? So many questions! I realise that something must be done for him. Most of all, it is the painting itself which fascinates me.

Could he really have contrived to paint my fortune? And his own future days into the bargain? What else was there that I hadn't had time to see or make out?

I realise that something must be done for him. From the story told on the walls it is clear this Buryatin is someone from the old days. An old Party member? Should I find out from Uncle if he is facing arrest? That would be to draw attention to him. As it is he is fading from everyone's memory. If he is not in some sort of trouble, why else would he be hiding? I will decide on all of this at some other time. First and foremost, something needs to be done about the paintings, about the whole apartment. A man's secret thoughts on display like that would land him in a mess of trouble.

The next morning, though still feeling weak, I discharged myself from the tiny hospital and immediately headed to the maintenance store, down in the basement. I spent a good hour sorting out everything I would need and got one of the men from the boiler room to help me carry it all up to the 9th floor. Then I began to paper over the entire flat. It felt like, I don't know, some kind of a desecration but I knew that if I did not do this now, Dubkhov would have me painting over it (or even worse), washing it off the walls soon enough. By papering I knew that the paint would be less damaged and the images probably much better preserved. When this is all done, then I can figure out just what to do about this Buryatin. It took me two days working flat out and late into the night (the ceiling as well!) and it has nearly done for me. I feel terribly weak. No sign of any more n.b.'s yet though.

Thankfully, the carpet had all been kept, several big rolls were left in the bedroom as well as most of the furniture, chairs, tables, even paintings for the walls! All of this I put back when I had finished the papering, just to complete the picture. The whole process was intensely demoralising, it felt like reverse archaeology, but I am utterly certain it was something that had to be done.

By early evening on the second night I had finished and, though I was weak, tired and terribly nervous, I knew that now was the time to confront Buryatin and, if I could, to try and figure out a way to help him. I turned the key and slowly entered the flat. But of Valentin Buryatin, there was no sign.

THE MIRACLES

#1. THE CELL

My selfe being bound up against a wall in a dark & most noisome cell did cry out boldley for succour & none being forthcoming did readily despair for fearing that the time was near come upon me to be delivered unto Him My God the Father I cried for why had he forsaken me my breath did come in never more than short fits & startes & the terrible thought that I would soon meet my end in this most heinous place at first assaulted my poor brain then did of a sudden o'ertake my bodily frame in prodigious damp sweats & a shaking palzy the pain in my ankles my balles & in my hands was unbearable & from the vaults & pens around me, the only sounds in my ears were the miserable crying & screaming of men & women I found myself fading in & out of consciousness & truly reckoned my final hour was pending in the midst of this apocalypse of fear & cruelty how did I come to be here? I thought myself better fitted for long life & a gentle olde age having lived a righteous & most Godly existence heretofore & so it was at this hour that the True Saints came upon me in my cell who would sayve me & shew me the way to my freedom towards which they took me down from the hooke on the wall & took the gagg from my mouth then they eazed some of the paine from around my testackles & from my ankles in a most mirakulous way & then these silent helpers used magick rodds to soothe my head & the softe partes of my feet & indeed they were more akin in their actions to magicians rather than to mere apothekaries though notwithstanding this they all wore masques oh & would that I could but of seen their faces to thank them though at the time I verily believed they were little less than angels though they clothed themselves in the black garb of asasins then they did take me to a machine to alleveate the paine in my dislocated ankles & arms which device did relocate those various limbes into their true sockets & I praised almighty God for this miracle & they then took me to another more commodious cell where they did remove many of the burns & nasty bruises from my poor body the first by means of a miraculous cauterisation wherein hot pokers were used in a most ingenious way to remove the blisters the second by means of the balming rodds they had used upon me at first & forthwith after another fewe lonely moments in the cell, my final meeting with my saviours relieved me of the last of my paine when they undertook to massage my whole frame most comfortably with their feet as I lay prone upon the floore at last a black cloth bagge or heavy blindfold was placed over my head dowtless to protect further the identity of my saintly friends & I was led out from my cell down some steps & into a coach & from here I was driven across the city & back to the doore of my home where *in fine* the blindfold was released from my eyes and my secret saviours drove off into the night God bless them these Christian men & may His name be praized in all his mercifulness!

#2. THE FIRE.

The first to appear before the Council was Signor Trontii a wineseller of this town. Having been sworn, Signor Trontii then bore witness to the assembly that he had, with his own eyes *"given him by Almighty God"*, witnessed the incredible phenomenon of Maria-Theresa Larenzini, walk free from a huge bonfire in the Campo of this town on the early morning of September 5th, 1654. The Archbishop asked Signor Trontii to explain the circumstances of this supposed incident. Signor Trontii continued by saying that he had seen the flames of a *"raging"* fire which the population of the town had come across, quickly recede and eventually extinguish altogether, the last of the embers being put out by one of the soldiers. And that then Maria-Theresa Larenzini had been helped down from the stake to which she had been tied over the piles of dry sticks and faggots of wood and into a tumbrel, from whence she was slowly taken out of sight of himself and of the crowd and behind the walls of the prison. His Holiness The Archbishop then asked Signor Trontii whether he would consider his story fanciful were he to hear it from any other mouth but his own. Signor Trontii replied that it would surely sound to him like the most ridiculous fabrication he had ever heard. Nevertheless, he continued, was not the evidence of these his eyes enough. Signor Trontii asserted that it was not every day one witnessed a miracle and should His Holiness wish for corroboration he should ask any of the other good people of Basanto assembled here before him. He petitioned His Holiness in the name of the people of Basanto that Maria- Therese would be granted the sainthood she most obviously warranted by this blessed Council. His Holiness thanked the witness for his testimony and said the question of sainthood was yet to be approved but that was under the direct consideration of the Council.

#3. RESURRECTION IN ALFÁCAR

As I told you, at that time I was working as a trainee teacher at Alfácar. I was young; I think I must have been about seventeen, and these were interesting times, you know? Every day bought news of more fighting, we were all pretty scared. You never knew who would be in control from one day to the next and those with strong views on one side or the other, affiliations, loyalties; well they were always worried. I suppose because they had the most to lose, no?

Anyway, on this one day, I think it was in August, anyway it was summer and there was some big commotion in the area of Viznar. We had heard all sorts of rumours throughout the day but that was nothing out of the ordinary, believe me! By the evening everyone was so scared that most of us were staying inside. In those days, small problems in Viznar became big problems in Alfácar very quickly!

As it happened, that night I had no choice but to travel to the house of my fiancé at Jun. Her old grandfather was ill, I think with some fever and so I had picked up the medicine that afternoon from Signor Reyes' the farmacéutico in Alfácar. So, about halfway along as I was crossing the main road (the Granada road) on the way to Jun, a car passed me going very fast; I remember because I came off the road (I was on my new bicycle) and nearly went into a ditch. Then a lorry came up. The driver had seen me, and they stopped. A tall man got out of the passenger side. It was dark but I could tell he was an important man. I could see he had a pistol in a holster and I was starting to get pretty scared, even though I had done nothing wrong and had, at that time, no real political thoughts or...affiliations. I thought he might be Falange but I was not really sure. What would such a person look like? He could just as easily of been a banderillero. Who could tell? Our village was small and these were still early days. So this fellow steps up in a real hurry and straight away asks me if I am loyal to Spain! That's not a good start! Not a fair question, uh? What am I supposed to say? No? He says that they need my help urgently and would I be prepared to come with them? Of course my eye kept returning to that holster! I said of course I would help them but I can tell you I did not want to get involved. What choice did I have? The big man asked me to step up into the back of the truck which I did and there were three other men in the back of the truck, none of whom I knew, at least they weren't from my village. So, then away we went down the road, hell-for-leather! Within a few minutes the truck pulled up at the side of the road behind that car that I had seen first of all. The whole time I never saw anyone get out from that car which I remember because it looked like quite a new Citroen. A beautiful car! I was not sure where we were exactly, I knew the whole area pretty well but I was scared and confused, remember, and it was a dark night. And hot! Whew! There were a lot of olive trees, but so what? The back of the truck came down and the men helped me down. Most of them were carrying lanterns and the big man in the front had an electric torch. I asked the man next to me what was going on but he just told me to shut my mouth and do as I was told!

So anyway we walked across the road, through these olive trees and halfway into a field. By this time let me just say that my heart was going ten to the dozen! I had heard a lot about the paseos[24] on both sides though most of it then was just so much talk, a lot of rumours. I had found it all difficult to believe. But as I walked into that field I really thought hard about those rumours I can tell you! Anyway a few steps further on and I noticed a lot of disturbed earth, like someone had been digging there recently. This sight did not help my state of mind at all, señor! I was getting more and more nervous. The men I was with were in a real hurry and when they had found these patches of earth, they immediately set about digging, but with a vengeance! The big man handed me a shovel and told me to dig too, which I immediately began to do. At this point, well, I was really shocked at what happened, I still remember it like it was yesterday. I could hardly believe what I saw but, there it was! The man digging to my left uncovered the face of a man! And, what I will never forget, still breathing! He had been buried alive here and very recently! The man was taken out of the hole he was in and he was in a really terrible state, of course! Terrible! His mouth, his eyes, his nose all were filled with earth. The one who had unearthed him set to bringing this man around, cleaning and wiping his face and clearing his air passages while the big hombre told the rest of us not to stop and to keep digging faster! And before I knew it there under my shovel, here was another body! I worked fast to uncover his face, which was lying straight down against the earth, but another man came over and after a real scramble we had freed him. I was convinced this one must be dead but after a few moments he started coughing, throwing up all this black soil! And he was alive! I dragged the poor cabrón up and over to the truck, he coughing and puking all the while and meanwhile two others had been found! Both alive! ¡Dios mío! I will never forget the first poor man's face! I even spoke to him a little while. He had no memory of who he was or how he got there! I asked him what scoundrels had done this to him but he had no notion. He was also bleeding from some head wound. Before I could ask him anything else the big hombre and the other men started hustling him and the other three into the back of the truck. I was bundled in too and they dropped me a mile or so up the road.

That was the last I saw of any of them.

#4. THE CHAIR

"Dateline Michigan. March 3rd. In all the long years this correspondent has worked in his own humble way on behalf of this newspaper to 'shine forth the light of truth' into the homes of Our Great Nation, never before has his credulity been put to a stricter or more rigorous test than yesterday afternoon in downtown Michigan at the Grand Unveiling of a New Wonder Cure…."

It was a March morning like a hundred others. The sun took one doubtful look, thought to itself: What the Hell? and let itself be slowly covered in a smear of cloud, like wet cement around a mobster's spats. An hour later and the cab was pulling up outside Michigan State. I put the bill down on the company tab. Jerry (my photographer) and I shared a quick smoke and then walked up the wide marble University steps and into Reception.

I had to admit to more than a passing interest in the story. There must have been some kind of foul-up on the paperwork because usually it was that jerk Fernando who got all the good staff stories. Why the stars shone for me that day? Who knew? Maybe Fernando had a headache? Maybe they had me down as the scientific type? Either way there we were and not short on company. Almost all the staff hacks I knew were messing up the place, plus a lot of out-of-town boys. Chicago, Detroit, New York. You could cut the hair-oil and cheap bourbon atmosphere with a bent Press Pass. Crumpled suits, dog-eared ties, work-all-night eyes and *way* too much coffee. Several of my esteemed colleagues there assembled had been playing down the rumours of a new wonder cure emanating from the government scuttlebutt. Me, I had always tried to keep at least a halfways open mind. But the truth is, nothing could have prepared any of us for what was to come.

After a couple of minutes, the Director appears amid all the commotion, along with his Chief Scientist: one Professor Elbers. A few premature flashbulbs blew but Jerry was biding his time. A brief introduction from the Director, then Elbers took the helm. He was a pretty cool customer. Austrian. No duelling scar but frosty blue eyes behind the tan. He began to tell us that today we were the first privileged few to be part of a new and truly seismic development in the field of medicine. For too long, said Elbers, science has stumbled in the darkness. Today, a new light, a bright electric light will be turned on and nothing, nothing will ever be the same again.

The room was suddenly a lot quieter. Admittedly we jaded Gentlemen of The Fourth Estate had all heard this type of thing before from all kinds of salesmen: politicians, the Mayor's Office, Big Business, but this time, something in those ice-blue eyes had the air of real conviction. My palms were beginning to get a little sweaty.

Introductions over, we were now, all of us: led out by the Director and Herr Elbers, down a set of stairs and along a long corridor, across a damp courtyard to a squat, nondescript building separated from the rest of the campus. Here our passes were studiously rechecked.

Along another corridor into a large empty room marked TEST CHAMBER #1 with a huge glass partition at the other end. Through that, we could see three lab-coated scientists operating a large bank of electrical equipment. Thick wires and conduit, flashing lights and circuitry (all the usual doohickies) and there, on a small dais in the middle of the room was a large, black chair. It looked ominous, like a torture device, with leather thong at wrist and ankle and several thick, red wires coming out of its base. The atmosphere had been a little tense over in reception, now everyone was subdued and getting increasingly nervous, including myself. The smell in their was unsettling, like overcooked fat and gunpowder.

Finally Prof. Elbers, whom no-one had seen slipping away, suddenly materialised in a white coat, on the other side of the screen. He picked up a large microphone, like the type they have at Radio City. Gentlemen, he began, we have christened it the LAZARUS DEVICE and after seven years of top-secret research, it is now my proud duty to show this prototype to you, the eyes of the world. Two more white-coated assistants then wheeled something in on a gurney, covered in a mint green sheet. Elbers then asked if a Dr. Spatzky was in the audience. Some old guy who I hadn't noticed put up his hand and was led through another door into the Test Room. As soon as the old guy got in there, Herr Elbers, somewhat theatrically, whipped off the sheet to reveal a dead man on the gurney. Age about thirty five to forty, shaven headed and naked as a babe. Prof. Elbers then asked Spatsky (which gentleman, explained Elbers, was a recognised authority on Pathology and Forensic Science) to examine the corpse. This the rather embarrassed figure of Spatzky did. Elbers then had him give his verdict over the microphone which fed back slightly as he pronounced the man quite dead. The Doc was hustled back in with us by two of Elbers assistants and now, said Elbers, we can begin the demonstration. He stepped over to the bank of circuitry while his assistants manoeuvred the corpse of the man into position, off the gurney and into the chair. They strapped him in with those leather belts around wrists, ankles and neck, then tied a wet sponge around the top of his head and electrodes to his temples and his chest. Then, after a brief speech from Elbers (which I don't think any of us heard, or at least could not remember afterwards), he threw the switch. All the lights appeared to dim for a moment and a strange, unearthly glow filled the Test Chamber.

I could taste iron filings at the back of my mouth. All of us watched for long minutes in horror, until – what I still cannot believe I saw – the fingers of the corpse began to quiver! Next, his neck and head and then the rest of his body fell to shaking, only a little at first, then more and more violently until now he was shaking and jolting about like a crazy doll. Even from where we were stood one could watch the currents of electricity visibly pass across his muscles. It made me sick to watch it. At last, when the whole ungodly scene felt like it was reaching such a zenith that the poor sap might be torn to pieces, his eyes suddenly opened. The same guinea pig: only minutes ago, a carcass on a slab and as stiff as an old board was staring wild-eyed across the room towards us. Towards me.

The switch was thrown at last and the guinea pig fell back into the chair, for all the world, dead once again. But the assistants had already begun to unstrap him from the chair and he slowly raised his head as they lifted him out and, supporting him under each arm, led him to the centre of the chamber. All the while, ever since the machine had stopped, Dr. Spatzky's voice had been echoing around the room: No! No! he cried over and over again. Two more of the white coats came in and helped the Doctor out of the room.

I thought it was the beads of sweat that had been coursing down my face since the demonstration began, then, when I wiped my face with a handkerchief, I realised they must have been tears.

NOTES

1 *Admiral Aleksandr Vasiliyevich Kolchak.* (1874-1920) Leader of anti-Bolshevik (White) forces during the Russian Civil War (1917-1923)

2. *Mikhail Nikolayevich Tukhachevsky* (1893-1937) Soviet military commander and Marshal of the Soviet Union. Executed during the Great Purge (1937-39)

3. *Kulaks* were a class of prosperous Russian peasant, widely persecuted, especially by Stalin during the process of collectivisation (1929-40)

4. *Nikolai Ivanovich Bukharin* (1888-1938) Highly influential early Bolshevik political leader and chairman of *Comintern* (Communist International). An opponent of Stalin, he was executed during the Great Purges after a show trial.

5. The *NKVD* or People's Commissariat for Internal Affairs made up the secret and public police force that operated during the Stalin years. It was preceded by the *Cheka* and the *OGPU*. When the NKVD disbanded in 1946, its operations were taken over by the *KGB*.

6. A *verst* is an obsolete Russian measure of distance equivalent to 3500 feet or 1.067 kilometers.

7. *Kazimir Severinovich Malevich.* Russian Supremacist painter. (1879-1935)

8. *The Lubyanka,* a notorious prison on Lubyanka Square, Moscow, was also the headquarters of the secret police (Cheka, NKVD and KGB)

9. *Tsar Nicholas II* (1894-1918) and his entire family were executed by a Bolshevik firing squad at Ipatiev House, Yekaterinburg on the night of the 17th July 1918.

10. *Arbat Street* is a famous pedestrian street in central Moscow.

11. *Vsevolod Emilevich Meyerhold* (1874.1940?) Highly influential Russian theatre director, actor & impresario. Founded his own theatre in 1922. Tortured and then executed during the Great Purges.

12. *Baron Roman Nikolai Maximilian von Ungern-Sternberg* (1886-1921) was the self-declared dictator of Mongolia during the Russian Civil War. His armies fought with the Whites against the Bolsheviks.

13. *The Five Finger Mountain* is a mountain of solid rock in the South Caucasus, in what is now Azerbaijan.

14. *Nikolai Ivanovich Yezhov* (1895-1940) was the infamousPeople's Commissar for Internal Affairs at the NKVD. Under Stalin's direct orders he was responsible for many hundreds of thousands of executions, interrogations and arrests. He was only five feet tall.

15. *Lazar Moiseyevich Kaganovich* (1893-1991) Soviet politician, encouraged and implemented widescale economic suppression of kulaks *(see above)*

16. *Jaan Anvelt* (1884-1937) was the Estonian Bolshevik leader who organised the successful uprising in Talinn at the time of the October Revolution in Russia (1917)

17. *Peredelkino* is a compound of '*dachas*' (country houses)

near Moscow, which became a writer's colony during the Stalin era. Former residents included Boris Pasternak (1890-1969) Isaak Babel (1894-1940) and Mikhail Bakhtin (1895-1975)18. *The Revolutionary Insurgent Army of the Ukraine* or *Black Army* was an anarchist peasant army that fought a guerilla campaign against the White Army in the Russian Civil War. They were led by Nestor Ivanovych Makhno (1888-1934) as a protest against the oppression of the workers and peasants by the bourgeois-landlord authority on the one hand and the Bolshevik-Communist dictatorship on the other. During a brief period in the conflict they established an independent anarchist state in the Ukraine.

19. A *tachanka* is a horse drawn machine gun.

20. A *shaska* is a Caucasian sword favoured by the Cossacks.

21. *The Great Siberian Ice March* (1920) During the Russian Civil War, when the White Army, retreating East along the Trans Siberian Railway, crossed Lake Baikal into China, in the depths of the Russian winter. Thousands perished in the cold and were left where they died until the spring thaws, when their bodies sank into the lake.

22. *The Schwanengesang* (Swan Song) is a cycle of songs by the German composer Franz Schubert (1797-1828)

23. *The Tenth Party Congress* was held in 1921 and decided many aspects of Lenin's NEP (New Economic Policy)

24. A *paseo* ('short walk') was a euphemism for summary, usually roadside, executions carried out by both sides in the Spanish Civil War (1936-39)

OTHER TITLES FROM LENZ BOOKS

FICTION
BYSTANDERS: HER BERLIN NOTEBOOK
MIRJAM HADAR MEERSCHWAM

MY LIFE WITH BELLE
JUDITH RAVENSCROFT

ART
FIFTY DRAWINGS
TIMOTHY HYMAN

PAINTING: MYSTERIES AND CONFESSIONS. A COLLECTION OF WRITINGS
TESS JARAY

www.lenzbooks.com